Josiah Strong, James H Ross

A Martyr of To-Day

The life of Robert Ross, sacrificed to municipal misrule, a story of patriotism calling

for municipal reforms

Josiah Strong, James H Ross

A Martyr of To-Day
The life of Robert Ross, sacrificed to municipal misrule, a story of patriotism calling for municipal reforms

ISBN/EAN: 9783337309756

Printed in Europe, USA, Canada, Australia, Japan

Cover: Foto ©Raphael Reischuk / pixelio.de

More available books at **www.hansebooks.com**

A MARTYR OF TO-DAY.

THE

LIFE OF ROBERT ROSS,

SACRIFICED TO MUNICIPAL MISRULE,

A Story of Patriotism

CALLING FOR MUNICIPAL REFORMS.

BY

REV. JAMES H. ROSS.

WITH AN INTRODUCTION BY

REV. JOSIAH STRONG, D.D.

AUTHOR OF "OUR COUNTRY," "THE NEW ERA," ETC.

ILLUSTRATED.

BOSTON:
JAMES H. EARLE, PUBLISHER,
178 WASHINGTON STREET.
1894.

CONTENTS.

PREFATORY NOTE.

THIS volume is the outgrowth of an article by its author, in *The Golden Rule*, Boston, Mass., entitled "A Martyr to Pure Politics." The publisher of this book saw in that article the germ of a book of national importance and interest, and requested the author, Mr. Ross, to write it.

The martyrdom of Robert Ross, and its meaning, have been commented upon in the daily and weekly press of the nation. For the sake of accuracy, and out of love for the deceased, the family designated their pastor, the undersigned, to furnish Mr. Ross with the materials available for the publisher's purposes, because he was born and bred in Troy, bears the family name, and could be trusted to do justice to his theme. He alone is responsible for the form of the narrative, and for any expressions of opinion that it may contain.

It is believed that the pure, symmetrical life of

Robert Ross will exert a wholesome influence
wherever the record of it becomes known; that
it cannot fail to interest all organizations of young
people, secular and religious, such as the athletic,
Sabbath schools, the Brotherhood of Andrew and
Philip, the Young Men's Christian Association,
and the Endeavor Societies; that the present
revival of public interest in municipal conditions,
problems, and reforms, by Lyceum and Municipal
Leagues, various civic clubs and societies, cannot
be stimulated in any better way than by noting
the situation in Troy as typical and crucial.
Troy has been misgoverned. Reforms are now
attempted. If successful, there is no city in the
land that will not acquire new hope and courage;
for the task is as difficult as can be found anywhere. The undersigned, in the address he gave
at the funeral of the deceased, said what he wishes
to reiterate, —

" THE DEATH OF ROBERT ROSS LEAVES WITH
US A LESSON AS CHRISTIANS AND CITIZENS. IT
IS THAT A MAN CAN BE A THOROUGHLY GOOD
CHRISTIAN, AND AT THE SAME TIME A GOOD
CITIZEN; AND, FURTHERMORE, THAT HE CANNOT

BE A GOOD CITIZEN WITHOUT BEING A CHRIS-
TIAN. . . . IT IS NOT UNMANLY TO BE A DE-
VOTED FOLLOWER OF JESUS CHRIST."

In behalf of George Ross and family.

WILLIAM H. SYBRANDT.

OAKWOOD MANSE, TROY, N.Y.

ACKNOWLEDGMENTS.

THE AUTHOR desires to tender his sincere and hearty thanks to the parents and brothers of ROBERT ROSS for photographs used in this biography, and to the Rev. WM. H. SYBRANDT as their prompt and efficient representative in communicating details ; to Secretary FOSTER TURNER, of the Esek Bussey Fire Engine Company, for photograph of the draped engine-house, and for correspondence ; to the *Troy Times* for reports of the murder and trial of the murderer, a verbatim report of the address to the jury of Attorney GEORGE RAINES of Rochester, N. Y., and for the plates loaned the publisher ; to *The Telegram*, of Troy, for a verbatim report of the address of the Rev. HERBERT C. HINDS ; to the Rev. JOSIAH STRONG, D. D., for his note of introduction ; and to numerous friends and editors who have encouraged the writing of the biography.

Gratefully,

JAMES II. ROSS.

BOSTON, MASS., 1894.

8

INTRODUCTION.

O NE of the most hopeful signs of the times is the widespread revival of civic patriotism.

Our most friendly critics abroad and our most intelligent citizens at home alike recognize in the government of our large cities the one conspicuous failure of our institutions; and this national disgrace is rapidly becoming a national peril. The question whether the city is capable of self-government involves the question of national self-government, for the city is soon to dominate the nation.

At present the state does not trust the city to govern itself; it is the state which determines to what extent the city shall manage its own affairs. But soon the city will take matters into its own hands, and control, not only its own affairs, but those of the state and of the nation also. The wonderful growth of our cities during recent years is not local nor temporary. It is not due to the

peculiar conditions of a new civilization. It is a
world phenomenon, and is due to causes which
enter as essential elements into modern civilization everywhere; and as these causes are permanent, there can be no reasonable doubt that this
tendency from country to city will be permanent.
Our urban population is now six times as large as
it was forty years ago, and relative to the whole
population it is more than twice as large. From
1880 to 1890 our rural population increased only
fourteen per cent, while our urban population increased sixty-one per cent. If this rate of increase
continues for a quarter of a century, in 1920 our
urban population will be upwards of ten millions
greater than our rural. If the city is incapable
of self-government then, as it is now, what will
become of state and nation when it dominates
them both ?

Our American institutions are based on two
fundamental principles which are co-ordinate and
alike essential; viz., local self-government and
federation. The latter was at stake in the civil
conflict of a generation ago, and was immovably
established by the result of the war. The other
principle is now on trial, and it is yet to be deter-

mined whether a large city population is capable of self-government. On that issue, as we have already seen, depends the permanence of our free institutions.

We need, therefore, a new patriotism which is civil rather than military, which fixes its attention, not on the Union, which is no longer imperilled, but on local government, which has become widely corrupted — not a patriotism which constructs fortifications and builds navies (though with the present degree of civilization these may still be needed), so much as one which purifies politics and substitutes statesmen for demagogues; not one which follows the drum-beat to battle, but one which goes to primaries; not one that "rallies round the flag" so much as one that rallies round the ballot-box; not a patriotism which exhausts itself in eulogizing our institutions, but one which expresses itself in strengthening their foundations.

Such patriotism calls for courage no less than that which devotes itself to military service. It calls for men brave enough to face the hatred of pothouse politicians, who are as mean as they are unscrupulous; it calls for men who dare to be unpopular, who dare to be misunderstood and misrepresented ; men who dare to be ridiculed and lied about and abused ; men who dare to suffer in their business, and, if need be, in their bodies ; men who can wait for justification because they are working, not for applause, but for principle.

Such was the young man the story of whose martyrdom is told in this book. He was as true a patriot and hero as if he had fallen on the field of battle. Not many like Robert Ross will be called to resist unto blood, striving against municipal corruption ; but we need the same spirit of courage, of self-devotion, of intelligent patriotism, and the same largeness of mind which is capable of rising above all prejudice of party, race, and religion, if we are to stamp out the foul evils that are brooded by bossism.

Happily this new patriotism is rapidly growing. Its spirit is finding expression in many ways, one of the most significant of which is the good-citizenship movement of the Society of Christian Endeavor, of which young Ross was an active member. His early death was none too early, if the spirit of Christian patriotism which animated him becomes thereby the inspiration of a host of American youth.

The biographer of Robert Ross, though bearing the same family name, is not a relative. His pen has been inspired, not by any personal motive, but by interest in municipal reform, to which cause this volume is calculated to render eminent service.

JOSIAH STRONG.

Father of Robert Ross.

A MARTYR OF TO-DAY.

CHAPTER I.

PARENTAGE AND PUPILAGE.

OVER the pavilion, on the left of the visitor, as he entered the Administration Building of the World's Fair, in Chicago, 1893, was an ideal and allegorical statue entitled "Strength." It consisted of two youthful figures, male and female. The name would seem to have been due to the male figure only. He was represented as seated, and he was the model of a modern trained athlete. His figure was imposing, his face was that of a youth conscious of his strength, eager for the exertion of his powers, and his attitude that of affection and protection for the woman who leaned upon him confidingly, and whom he covered with his broad shield.

The statue was one of many intended to illustrate the characteristics and virtues of Americans.

Not only physical strength, but moral courage
was typified. The face was intellectual. There
was in it the expectancy that anticipated a coming
adversary, against himself or the woman by his
side, or against both. No fear was apparent, no
prophecy except an assurance of perfect safety
and complete victory.

If the statue had attempted to portray Robert
Ross and his betrothed on the very eve of their
marriage, and of his death by violence, it could
scarcely have been more accurate. He was murdered March 6, 1894, and was to have been
married in May. If some image-breaker like Mo-
hammed had broken the statue into fragments,
suddenly and with one blow, he would have represented the murderer, who, by taking the life of
Robert Ross, transformed a romance into a tragedy, and a private life into a public one attaching
itself to great governmental problems and reforms.
The same over-ruling Providence that changed the
Cross as a symbol of shame into a symbol of glory,
hallowed his name, glorified his death, and transfigured his life.

The circumstances that attended his death disclosed a youth of rare qualities, one upon whose

entire career the search-light of publicity, legal
scrutiny, and ingenious, fertile hostility has been
turned, revealing nothing that discredits him and
much that elevates him above many youth of kindred years and station in life. He was strong and
safe as a boy and a youth. Nature endowed him
with physical powers and moral qualities that
made him self-reliant, a help to the weak and the
timid, an example alike to the class of youth that
strive for moral mastery of themselves and to
those who surrender to temptations, vices, and
crimes. In life and death he did the state a mani-
fold service, which has been and will be recognized
and honored in various ways.

The genealogical and national fountains out of
which his life issued must be opened, or his life
and his victory in death cannot be comprehended.
They flowed from the Highlands and Lowlands of
old Scotland. He was of Scotch descent, from
both parents.

His father, George Ross, was born in Prestonpans, Scotland, which is on the Firth of Forth in
the western part of the County of Haddington.
The tradition of the origin of the name of Prestonpans is that it was first called Priest-toon

because of a little colony of Roman Catholic priests living there. It was also called " The Pans," from the pans used in evaporating the salt water. The two names were finally combined into Prestonpans.

It is eight and one-half miles east of Edinburgh, and participates therefore in the influences that radiate from that terraced, beautiful, and cultured city, that many regard as the most beautiful city in the world.

The whole region is historic. Scotland and Prestonpans shared in the witchcraft delusion of the seventeenth century. In 1607 Isobel Grierson was burned at Prestonpans, on the ground that, in the house of Adam Clark, in the likeness of his own cat, she had frightened his household and especially his maid-servant. She had also disturbed by her enchantments the family of a man named Brown, to whom she appeared as "ane infant bairn."

· During the English Revolution of 1603 to 1658, Oliver Cromwell defeated at Prestonpans, in 1648, a Scotch army led into England by the Duke of Hamilton to help Charles the First, who reigned from 1625 to 1649.

A war between France and England induced France, in 1744, to place Prince Charles Edward Stuart, grandson of James II., at the head of the Jacobites, and a formidable armament. The Jacobites were the adherents of the male line of the house of Stuart in Great Britain. In 1745 the youthful adventurer, who sought to recover the throne of his royal ancestor, landed in a small vessel, with only seven friends, on a little island of the Hebrides. Soon some of the Scotch Highland chiefs pledged themselves to support his cause with their substance and followers.

Many, however, stood aloof, or sustained the opposing side, under the leadership of the Lord President, Duncan Forbes Stewart of Culloden. Sir John Cope marched his royal troops northward to Inverness, thereby avoiding rather than encountering the opposing forces. On the 17th of September the rebels marched into Edinburgh, and proclaimed James the Pretender, father of Edward, at the Town Cross, as King. They obtained weapons and ammunition that had been stored to defend the city against them. Then they won an easy victory over Sir John Cope at Prestonpans. A single charge of the clansmen

cut to pieces his two thousand British troops,
and led to the capture of their cannon, baggage,
and military chests. From the church steeple of
the village, Rev. Alexander Carlyle [1722–1805]
had seen Prince Edward enter Edinburgh, and had
watched the battle, in which the gallant Colonel
Gardiner fell, with whom the Scotch village
parson had dined the previous day. There is a
monument to Colonel Gardiner at the appropriate
spot.

Prestonpans to-day is devoted to the manufac-
ture of salt by evaporation. It is supposed to
have had salt pans as early as the 12th century,
and thriving manufactures until some time after
the Reformation. The population is commercial
and sea-faring. There is an old ruined castle outside of the village. The house known as "Colonel
Gardiner's house" stood about half a mile south
of the castle. An old thorn-tree southeast of
Prestonpans is still pointed out as marking the
spot where the battle was hottest. There is also
a high wall standing there which was a barrier to
those escaping from the pursuers, and where a
great many were slain. A stone staircase remains, but all the woodwork of the structure was

long ago destroyed by fire. The grounds, covering five or six acres, and enclosed by a stone wall six or seven feet high, contain apple and pear trees, and are cultivated as a garden, the products of which are sent to the Edinburgh market.

The clan of Ross represents the best Scottish blood and history. It is traceable to the Scotch Highlands. The meaning of the word Ross is promontory or headland. The Scotch race are identical historically with the Irish. They are the remnant of the great Celtic race that the Roman and Saxon invasions of Scotland on the south, and the Danish invasions from the east and the west, did not touch. They were the last to resist with success the almost uniformly conquering armies of Rome.

In the year 81 A.D., North Britain was inhabited by twenty-one aboriginal tribes or clans. The clan system was a larger family system, the patriarchal form of government, manifesting natural authority, expressing and invoking affection and unqualified reverence for the supreme command. "The Highlander," says Professor John Stuart Blackie, himself a typical Scotchman, "was a healthy man, a sturdy peasant, a good workman, a natural gymnast, an intrepid fighter, a daring commander, and the best of colonists." In essentials the description applies to Robert Ross.

The origin of clanships and tartans is unknown. A map of Scotland, published in 1654, contained an ornamental title, representing two Highlanders in striped clothes, one wearing the " Belted Plaid," a large, long piece of plaiding, so folded and confined by a belt around the waist as to form a complete dress, plaid and kilt in one piece. That is assumed to have been the origin of the now highly ornamental Highland dress ; and if correct, the style is exactly two hundred and forty years old, or two centuries and two-score years.

Various colored cloths have been worn by the different clans of the Highlanders from a very early period. Originally tartans, the striped and spotted cloths, were worn only by native Highlanders ; and so the Lowlanders, the dwellers in the Border Counties on the south, and the dwellers in the northeast were excluded. More recently many tartans have been invented and manufactured.

The Highlanders have always been distinguished for *bravery*.

Mother of Robert Ross.

The clan of Ross began with Paul MacTire, famous in tradition for indomitable valor. To him William, Earl of Ross, Lord of Skye, granted a charter for the lands of Gairloch in 1366. Some authorities date the origin as far back as 1220, so that the history of the clan covers from five and one-quarter to six and three-quarters certuries. The Rosses of Balnagowan were a very ancient line, as they sprang from William, Earl of Ross, a great patriot and steady friend of King Robert I. Earl Hugh, the son of Earl William of Ross, was killed at Halidon Hill, while fighting for his king and country, in 1333.

Historically, therefore, Robert Ross and his murderer, through their remote ancestors, were natural allies by nationality. Religious dissensions had made those ancestors members of conflicting forms of religion, Roman Catholic and Protestant. The first great ecclesiastical struggle in Scotland was for the overthrow of Roman Catholicism, and accomplished its object. Inherited prejudices had made his assailant a representative of historic antagonisms between Catholics and Protestants.

George Ross, father of Robert, a descendant

from the Highlanders, a Lowlander by birth, before leaving Scotland, became engaged to Isabella Connell, who was born in Renton, in the county of Dumbarton, about fifty miles west of Edinburgh, and so also her early life was spent within the range of influences radiating alike from the Highlands and from Edinburgh. The two were born and lived in youth within sixty miles of each other.

George Ross came to the United States in 1851. His betrothed came in August, 1853; and they were married in Brooklyn, N.Y., August 26, by a Methodist pastor. They have had ten children, five sons and five daughters. William Ross was shot before Robert was, on the evil election day in Troy, March 6, 1894. Both were born in Troy : William, May 3, 1857, at 311 Ninth Street ; Robert, September 2, 1868, at 443 Tenth Street. Robert was the youngest son. The training of the several children, including that of these two sons, was given first at home, a religious and moral training, principally by the mother, as in most homes. The Scotch antecedents and traditions were a part of the family life; otherwise the parents would not have been true Scotch, but a

Robert Ross at four years.

Scotchman who forgets or disowns his native heath is a rarity indeed. No nationality exceeds his in loyalty to native land and history.

In 1877, when Robert was nine years old, the family went to Mitchell, Mitchell County, Iowa, where William was engaged in farming, having gone thither three years before. Robert remained on the farm three years. He attended the district school while there, and some amusing incidents are told of his love of fun. He was a mischievous, but not an ill-disposed boy. On one occasion he startled his female teacher by holding a live rabbit close to her ear; at another time he suspended a broom so that when the teacher opened the door to get it to sweep the schoolroom, after the pupils were dismissed, it would fall upon her. He and others waited after school to see the show and hear the teacher scream. While in the West all the children, except Robert, were members of a Good Templar's Lodge. Robert was then too young to join. The family expressed the temperance sentiments and participated in the agitations that led Iowa to adopt constitutional prohibition of the liquor traffic.

After Robert's return from the West he at-

tended, for a short time, the public schools of
Troy, and was a faithful student. He never went
beyond the Grammar department. One of his
teachers, Miss Sarah Lundy, remembers distinctly
how eager he was, when a pupil of hers in the
drawing-class, to get all the information he could
in that branch. She speaks of him as serious,
eager, and alert to gain knowledge. He was especially interested in drawing, because it would be
of service in his anticipated work as a machinist.

While attending school in Troy, like many other
boys, he "carried collars." He did a kind of
wholesale business in this line. He had a wagon,
and took a large number of baskets to the shops.
The linen collar and cuff and shirt industries of
Troy are among its leading manufactures.

His teacher in the Sabbath School of the Oakwood Avenue Presbyterian Church was Wm. S.
Van Vleck, who had great interest in Robert as
well as love for him, and spoke of him as "his
boy."

When Robert was about twelve years old, one
of the neighbors in Troy, who kept a cow, prom-
ised him half a bushel of cherries from the tree
if Robert would catch his calf for him, as no one

seemed to be able to do it. "Rob," or "Bob" as he was nicknamed, easily caught the calf, and with one hand on its head and the other on its tail, which he occasionally twisted, he made the calf go wherever he wished, and soon earned his basket of cherries.

The remote and immediate origin of Robert Ross, therefore, accounts for him fully, not merely in the earlier, but later stages of his short career. His Scotch ancestry, his religious parents and home, his pupilage in the public schools and in the Presbyterian Sabbath School, his training in the knowledge of the Bible as the great rule of human life and duty, his free contact with varying nationalities in a city and ward of the city proverbial for its mixed nationalities, at once developed and liberalized him. The finished result was *a model young man.* At his funeral, held in the Second Presbyterian Church, on Fifth Avenue, because of its central location and its large seating capacity, the Rev. Wm. H. Sybrandt, who had known him well during the latter half of his life, said :

"The Americanized, Christianized blood of a Scotchman flowed in his veins, and he was true to his God, his home, his church, and his country."

CHAPTER II.

SOCIAL LIFE AND BUSINESS CAREER.

THERE is a phase and period of each life that lies between the schools and one's home and occupation. It is that phase which allies the individual with his fellows, that recognizes social instincts and obligations. The physical inheritance of Robert Ross was splendid. When full-grown, he was six feet, two and one-half inches in height, weighed two hundred pounds, and was finely proportioned.

He has been compared to Bishop Phillips Brooks in two particulars — his statuesque figure, and the purity of his life. He had trained himself athletically. He was fond of all kinds of in-door and out-door sports, Scotch and American, such as the Caledonian games, rope-pulling as a test of strength, swimming, base ball, foot-ball, croquet, lawn tennis, gymnastics, etc. He was depended upon for feats demanding physical strength and athletic judgment and skill. It was

J. C. Ross.

Robert Ross.
Adam Ross, 2d.

William Ross.

natural and easy for him to respond to such demands. He led in sports. He induced those younger than himself to engage in them, and was their eager, willing instructor. The children at picnics found in him and in his leadership one of the pleasures of their outing. The lower floor of his home was a well equipped private gymnasium.

Not animalism but athleticism was the spirit of his physical life. He kept himself pure. He was free from physical vices, from the self-indulgence that is self-destroying. He refrained from the roughness and pugilism to which a robust physique may easily descend. He might have made an admirable Y. M. C. A. gymnastic instructor, because of his trained physical powers and dexterity, and his pronounced religious spirit.

In August, 1887, when he was only nineteen years of age, while taking a ride in beautiful Oakwood cemetery with his father, mother, and sister Maggie, the rear wheel of the carriage suddenly collapsed and a serious accident seemed imminent. Robert immediately jumped from the carriage and caught by the head the horse, which had begun to rear. With the other hand he took a firm

hold of one of the horse's forelegs and threw him.
A runaway was thus prevented, and none of the
party was hurt.   The horse and carriage belonged
to Eugene McClure, who played an unenviable
part in the election tragedy as a saloon-keeper
and alleged ally of repeaters in voting.   McClure
had painted the wagon so that its defects were
concealed, although he must have known that
it was unsafe.

About two years ago, while Robert was putting a water engine in a church, he got into
very close quarters.   He had cut an opening in
the side of the pulpit platform just large enough
to admit his body by entering head first, but he
found after he had gone in that he was unable
to back out.   He was all alone, and as he could
make no one hear him he had either to help himself out or remain a prisoner.   His ingenuity,
however, suggested a way of egress, and his per-
severing will effected a release.   Taking his saw,
which he had fortunately carried in with him, he
reached back and sawed off a timber behind him,
and thus made a safe retreat.

The Ross Valve Company belongs to the New
England Water Works Association, which has

active and associate members. Last year, 1893,
while Robert was in Worcester, Mass., two base
ball nines were made up one day, one nine consisting of active members and the other of associate members. The nine to which he belonged, consisting of associate members, was
victorious.

" Rob " knocked the ball away off into a body
of water, and made the only home run that was
made.

His school life was short. His tastes were
mechanical. They were revealed early in life,
and were gratified and cultivated while in the
intermediate school. They hastened his entrance
upon a business career. He became a mechanic,
a member of the Master Mechanics' Association,
which held its last annual meeting in Saratoga,
N. Y. The Association held a memorial service
in Congress Hall Hotel, Sabbath evening, June 17,
1894. The memorial services were presided over
by G. W. Morris, of Pittsburg, and the memorial
was read by M. N. Forney, of New York. The
religious services were conducted by the Rev.
Dr. Joseph Carey, rector of Bethesda Episcopal
Church, Saratoga, and Archdeacon of the Convo-

cation of Troy.   The Bethesda Church surpliced
choir, and Reeve's American Band, of Providence,
R.I., assisted in the exercises.   Robert Ross was
among those whose life and death were commem-
orated.

The hymns sung were : —

"Jesus Lover of My Soul."

"Nearer my God to Thee."

"Lead Kindly Light."

The railway officials and representatives of railway supply houses united in a resolution, which
said that his qualities were gradually bringing
him into prominence as a successful business man,
and added : " we look upon him as one who gave
all, even his own young life, to help win and maintain clean and honest government.   We recognize
and honor his high principles, his devotion to
duty, and his fearlessness in danger, which he
fully realized."

He was regarded as thoroughly efficient and
reliable.   His chief work in the later years of his
life consisted in putting motors into church build-
ings for pumping organs by water power.   He
was brought into contact with the representatives
of religious organizations.   Church committees,

Roman Catholic priests, Protestant pastors and rectors alike welcomed him as an agreeable man, a skilled and trustworthy mechanic, and an exemplar of religion and morality, whose influence over his fellow-workmen was wholly for good. As a business man, and a social companion, he had no difficulty in affiliating with Roman Catholics, nor with priests. Just before and after his death an attempt was made to create the impression that he was a bitter personal antagonist of Catholics. His opposition was to corruption in politics.

A Protestant and a Republican, he could work and vote at the polls for a Democrat and a Roman Catholic. Any opposition from Catholics to him as a Protestant issued from " the baser sort," who would discredit any religious organization.

Assistant District Attorney Fagan, who prossecuted Bartholomew Shea as the murderer of Robert Ross, said in his opening speech to the jury :

" As a member of the Roman Catholic Church, as one born and bred in the faith of that Church, I wish to enter a most determined and heartfelt protest against the attempt of this defendant, as shown by the insinuations of his counsel, to wrap himself up in the mantle of that great Church, and

to attempt to hide his blood-stained hands beneath
the royal purple of her robe. As a member of
the great Democratic party, I most earnestly protest against the effort of the defendant to clothe
himself in the mantle of that party, and to hide
his hands, stained as they are with the blood of
Robert Ross, in the robe of that party."

Certainly, Robert did not mix business and religion and Catholicism so as to defeat his own
legitimate objects, and the identical objects of
those whom he represented. He was companionable, receptive to proffered hospitality, silent
where controversy could easily be invited or pre-
cipitated ; diplomatic and wise in dealing with
men of varying habits, tastes, and opinions.

He often dined with Roman Catholic priests.
On one occasion he wanted a glass of milk, saw
none, and asked for it. The priest humorously
replied : " You'll get no milk here." A suggestive wink directed Ross's attention to the
side-board, where equally suggestive and filled
decanters told well enough what he might have to
drink. He finally took tea, thereby neither offending his host nor compromising himself as a
pledged total abstainer from intoxicating liquors
and a believer in absolute prohibition of the liquor
traffic.

Robert was a man of energy, a "hustler" as some would say. To miss a train might mean to him the loss of a day, and he was on the alert to save time and make the most of it. Having occasion to do some work in a town on the Hartford and New Haven Railroad, he gave up his checks and left orders to have his bags all ready for him when he should leave. At this station a fence separates the trains going in one direction from those going in another. When Robert arrived at the depot, after having finished his work in town, the south-bound train, which he was to take, was nearly ready to start, but his bags had not been cared for as he had ordered. He quickly climbed over the fence, got his bags and dropped them on the other side of the fence, between the fence and the train. Then he climbed over himself, and, standing on the car platform, reached down, got the bags, and placed them on the car; but in bending over to do this he lost several small articles from his coat pocket: he stepped quickly from the platform to pick them up, and at the same moment the train started; and as the space between it and the fence was very small, Robert's body was turned around by the moving car. He had presence of mind, however, to drop down at once, otherwise he would have been instantly killed, and to lie at full length beside the track between the fence and the train so that the steps of the cars passed over his head, and he thus escaped unharmed.

While putting an organ motor in a church in Williamsburgh, N.Y., he found that the plumbers had filled with pipes the place he needed, and so it was necessary to make another.

A member of the building committee, a German, came in while Robert was busy, and, being somewhat annoyed at what seemed to him a sort of iconoclastic work, said to him, with a brogue and a peculiar tone which Robert afterwards used to imitate, to the great amusement of his friends, " I see you're rippin' an' *tare*-in' away."

Robert was a salesman as well as a mechanic. He had tried on one occasion to sell an organ motor to a Roman Catholic priest, but the reverend gentleman would not purchase it, as he thought the price was too high. Robert finally made the price satisfactory, and then the priest told him to "peck away."

His last business letter from the Valve Com-

pany was an order relating to work in a Catholic
Church. He was accustomed to sign his business
letters as " Rob," or " Bob," but in this instance
wrote his name in full, as it is seen in connection
with his portrait.

He patronized the firm of A. Meekin & Co.,
King Street, Troy, in ordering printing. That
firm publishes a temperance and prohibition paper,
and in its issue for April, 1894, Mr. Meekin
said : —

" In business relations, we found him punctual
and exemplary. One trait will serve to illustrate
his thoughtfulness for others. While it is cus-
tomary in societies and churches for the chairman
of committee on printing to first order the work,
take a bill when completed and hand it to an au-
diting committee, through whose hands it must
pass in reaching the treasurer, who suits his convenience in paying it, necessitating a delay of
weeks and not infrequently of months, Robert
Ross always paid for work ordered by him, took a
receipted bill, and thus assumed responsibility for
its payment. One who has waited over a year for
the payment of a bill amounting to one dollar
knows how to appreciate this trait in his character."

Robert Ross was one of the charter members of
the Esek Bussey Fire Company, No. 8, which was
organized January 23, 1888. Thus he became a

fireman in his twentieth year. The company is a
volunteer organization ; named in honor of a business man who has been a Trojan practically all his
life, and whose stove works are near the home of
Ross, and the Fire Company. It was confirmed by
the common council of the city, June 20, 1890. An
honorable pride prevails in the northeastern section of Troy over the existence of this company,
and the value of its services to the city, — the
name it bears, the social conditions of the building, its cleanliness, its homelike parlor, and the
fraternity of its members.

Robert Ross's name has been reviewed by the
company in the light of his membership, from its
origin to his death. Secretary Foster R. Turner
writes that " his enemies can find no blot or stain
on his character."

He was a superb fireman, by virtue of his figure, strength, skill, perseverance, self-control, and
daring. He took a joke kindly, and ignored what
might offend others, when as sometimes hap-
pened and may happen anywhere, a joke was too
practical or personal, and remarks were made that
were stinging to a sensitive nature, whether so
intended or not.

It would not have been safe for most young men to pick a quarrel with him, with expectation that a personal encounter would ensue. He was so conscious that the offender would be the worse for it and so indisposed to quarrelsomeness and fighting, that his silence and inaction were easily comprehended and were not mistaken for cringing and cowardice. He was a Christian when he joined the company, and as a fireman he did not discredit his Christianity. He was sound, not only in faith, but in morals. He did not swear, and, aside from the moral wrong of profanity, was too much of a gentleman to be vulgar among gentlemen. He respected their rights no less than the rights of ladies. He did not acquire the careless habits of the users of tobacco, chewers and smokers, and therefore did not offend the sensibilities of those who, whether gentlemen or ladies, find cuspidors and all-pervading tobacco smoke an unnecessary evil, as tested by good taste and politeness. He could engage in exhausting labors and exposures to extreme heat and cold, and drenching rains, without resorting to alcoholic stimulants as an immediate refuge and a quack remedy for weakness and chills; a cure-all for real

or fancied ills of the flesh.   He was jovial, without being coarse.   As a young man among young
men he practised religion and morality so well,
that it was not necessary for him to preach much,
yet he agitated for good measures and causes.

   He was spared from death by an accident only
to die by violence less than three months later.
On Thursday, December 14, 1893, a fire broke out
in the store of J. M. Warren & Co., corner of
Broadway and River Streets, the very centre of the
business district of Troy.   A double alarm was
sounded at 2.21 P.M., and the signal tap announ-
cing that it was extinguished, at 2.30 A.M. of December 15.   It had lasted twelve hours.   During
its progress the officer in command ordered Foster R. Turner, the secretary of the Esek Bussey
Company, to pick out five men, and try to break
through the wall of the burning building.   Climb-
ing to the neighboring roof of the firm of Stark-
weather & Allen, the group of picked men began
work.   They worked long and hard but unsuccess-
fully, owing to the dense smoke which choked and
blinded them.   They gave out, and a fresh relay
was sent to take their places, among whom was
Robert Ross.   The fire in the meantime was

creeping slowly but surely into the building beneath them. By a determined effort on the part
of the men, the hole was at last broken through,
when the smoke became so dense, that they could
not see their associates at the pipes who were at
that time on the roof, stationed only ten feet
away. They started back from the wall but could
not see. Robert Ross approached, unconscious
of his danger, the edge of the roof; but others
apprehending it, drew him back and saved him
from stepping into mid-air. But for them he
would have fallen at least seventy-five or eighty
feet. As soon as the first hole through the wall
was broken, two streams were turned into the
building, stopping all further danger southward.
Another hole was cut and the streams divided,
and in about five hours the fire was out.

The members of the Esek Bussey Company, act-
ing under orders from the officer in command, had
accomplished the strategic and heroic work which
led to the extinction of the fire, and had arrested
its threatened extension.

On the evening of March 6, the day of Robert
Ross's martyrdom, about twenty of his fellow-
members in the Fire Company were grouped in

their building, enraged and outraged by the mui-
derous events attending the city election, that had
removed one of their own number, a man, a workman, a fireman, and a Christian whom they loved.
They were in a desperate frame of mind, obedient
to the law as citizens, yet eager that justice and
the penalties of broken law should overtake the
murderer. The neighborhood was the most ex-
cited part of a city aflame with indignation. The
man who would have lisped then an insinuation
against the name of Robert Ross probably would
have suffered violence at their hands. A few
days later, a Trojan attorney, George B. Wellington, addressed eight hundred men who, he said,
would have flung away their lives for the sake of
the martyr and the city, if anything could have
been gained by it.

The walls of the parlor of the Esek Bussey
Fire Company are decorated by a framed crayon
portrait of Robert Ross, donated to the company
by A. Alexander, of the Troy Portrait Company.
A photograph is presented herewith of the engine
house as draped in mourning for a suitable period
after the martyr's death, in honor, it may be said,
of the loss of the most valued member of the
company.

Building of the Esek Bussey Fire Engine Company.

Of which Robert Ross was a member.

On the eve of his death, Robert Ross was on the eve of his anticipated marriage to Miss Nellie May Patton, a member of a neighboring family in the section of the city where he resided. Hartley Coleridge [1796–1849], son of the English philosopher and poet, wrote an ode "On a Young Man Dying on the Eve of Marriage," which may rightly be recalled in its application to Robert Ross and his betrothed : —

" With contrite tears, and agony of prayer,
   God, we besought, thy virtuous youth to spare,
   And thought, oh ! be the human thought forgiven,
   Thou wert too good to die, too young for heaven; —
   Yet sure the prayers of love had not been vain,
   If death to thee wert not exceeding gain.

Tho' for ourselves, and not for thee we mourn,
   The weakness of our hearts thou wilt not scorn;
   And if thy Saviour's and thy Father's will,
   Such angel love permit, wilt love us still,
   For Death, which every tie of earth unbinds, '
   Can ne'er dissolve ' the marriage of pure minds.' "

CHAPTER III.

CONSECRATED TO CHRIST AND THE CHURCH.

THE fruit of training in a Christian home, permeated by the traditions, methods, and proverbial characteristics of Scotch Presbyterianism, ripened early in the personal life of Robert Ross. The Rev. George VanDeurs, who is still living in Philadelphia, was pastor of the family at the time of his birth. The Rev. Wm. H. Sybrandt, under whose ministry he united with the church, has no recollection of having spoken to the youthful parishioner on that subject. He had watched the development of an attractive youth, but before he was aware, Robert was ready for church membership, and voluntarily presented himself. The candidate met the Session of the Oakwood Avenue Presbyterian Church, October 7, 1885, and was received into full communion, and on the following Sabbath, October 11, made a public profession of his faith. The pastor's text that morning was Psalm 89:33: "Nevertheless my

Oakwood Avenue Presbyterian Church,

Of which Robert Ross was a member.

loving kindness will I not utterly take from him, nor suffer my faithfulness to fail." The theme considered was the " Faithfulness of God." It is a theme worth recalling in the light of the religious trust and faithfulness unto death of the solitary member thus received. He had been in the Sabbath School since childhood. He came into the church intelligently, deliberately, sincerely, and freely. He was always a faithful member of it, regular in his attendance morning and evening, and a liberal contributor to its support. His membership covered about eight and one-half years.

The church with which he united was organized and its edifice dedicated in the very year that he was born. It is on the corner of Tenth and Hoosick Streets in the northeastern and hilly part of the city. The manse adjoining it was built in 1892. In the belfry of the church is a memorial bell given by John Sherry, one of Troy's successful merchants, in memory of his wife. The bells manufactured in Troy are heard all over the world. In this city was cast the famous Liberty bell of the Chicago Exposition.

The life of the church and the life of Robert

were parallel, chronologically considered, down to
the date of his death. It was an off-shoot from
the First Presbyterian Church on First Street, and
had its origin in a Sunday-school formed on Tenth
Street by elder A. H. Graves of that church during the pastorate of the Rev. Marvin R. Vincent,
D.D., now professor in Union Theological Seminary, New York City, and the honorary pastorate
of the famous Rev. N. S. S. Beman, D.D.

George Ross, father of Robert, was one of the
seven deacons chosen when the church was
organized. He afterward served as an elder. Its
members belong to those whom Abraham Lincoln
honorably designated as " the plain people."

They are industrious, energetic, enterprising,
and prosperous. Robert was well aware of the
standing of all the churches in Troy, but he never
left Oakwood for a larger or richer church.

The Presbyterian churches of the city have
been strong in their " Young People's Christian
Unions" for numbers and work accomplished.
They have been reluctant or slow, because of this
fact, to re-organize as Societies of Christian Endeavor. The Union in the Oakwood Avenue
Church is an illustration of the rule. Robert

Ross identified himself with several organizations of young people in the church and in the city, for both sexes and for males only, such as the Union already referred to, the Brotherhood of Andrew and Philip, the Y. M. C. A., North Troy, and the R. R. Y. M. C. A. He was favorable to the reorganization of the Union as a Society of Christian Endeavor, which was effected November 23, 1893.

All the societies referred to are branches, subdivisions of the church, spiritual organizations for spiritual ends. They are ecclesiastical, not secular nor political. They are open to church-members only, as active members ; in effect open to all the young, save as differentiated by sex. They are not secret. Robert was an active member, a participant by accepting offices, engaging in public exhortation and prayer, contributing toward expenses and beneficences, and sharing the activities and responsibilities of varied forms of Christian work. Every Trojan who ever knew Henry Sherrill, of the Second Presbyterian Church, will think of the two as belonging to the same spiritual type.

The Brotherhood of Andrew and Philip is,

therefore, a young men's organization in the local
church, with national and inter-denominational
affiliations. It was organized in Reading, Penn.,
in May, 1888, by Rev. Rufus W. Miller; and in
the Oakwood Avenue Church in Troy, February
26, 1881. Robert joined it as a charter member.
It is religious, Christian, Protestant, denominational, and inter-denominational. Each denomi-
nation has its own Brotherhood, made up of the
chapters within its own body. No chapter can be
organized without the consent of the pastor or
officials in charge of a congregation.

Every man desiring to become a member must
pledge himself to obey the rules of the Brotherhood so long as he shall be a member. These
rules are the rule of prayer: to pray daily for the
spread of Christ's kingdom among young men and
for God's blessing upon the labors of the Brotherhood ; also the rule of service : to make an earnest
effort each week to bring at least one young man
within hearing of the Gospel of Jesus Christ as
set forth in the services of the church, young
people's prayer-meetings, and young men's Bible-
classes.

The object and rules were adopted from the

Brotherhood of St. Andrew, in the Protestant Episcopal Church.

The Badge is a button, made of various materials, but always in the colors red, orange, and black; the star being the symbol suggested by the

MOTTO OF THE BROTHERHOOD :

"𝔄𝔫𝔡 𝔱𝔥𝔢𝔶 𝔱𝔥𝔞𝔱 𝔟𝔢 𝔴𝔦𝔰𝔢 𝔰𝔥𝔞𝔩𝔩 𝔰𝔥𝔦𝔫𝔢 𝔞𝔰 𝔱𝔥𝔢 𝔟𝔯𝔦𝔤𝔥𝔱𝔫𝔢𝔰𝔰 𝔬𝔣 𝔱𝔥𝔢 𝔣𝔦𝔯𝔪𝔞𝔪𝔢𝔫𝔱; 𝔞𝔫𝔡 𝔱𝔥𝔢𝔶 𝔱𝔥𝔞𝔱 𝔱𝔲𝔯𝔫 𝔪𝔞𝔫𝔶 𝔱𝔬 𝔯𝔦𝔤𝔥𝔱𝔢𝔬𝔲𝔰𝔫𝔢𝔰𝔰, 𝔞𝔰 𝔱𝔥𝔢 𝔰𝔱𝔞𝔯𝔰 𝔣𝔬𝔯 𝔢𝔳𝔢𝔯 𝔞𝔫𝔡 𝔢𝔳𝔢𝔯."

DANIEL xii. 3.

The three colors in combination are derived from the national emblems of the countries in which the Protestant Reformation arose — Germany and Switzerland — and of the Netherlands, whose glorious eighty years' struggle for civil and religious freedom and for gospel truth was for the benefit of the whole world.

The chapter in the Oakwood Avenue Presbyterian Church has been accustomed to meet every Sabbath morning after the morning service and hold a prayer meeting. Robert Ross was present at the meeting held on the last Sabbath morning of his life, and knelt and offered prayer. His pastor's reminiscences are peculiarly interesting at this point.   Mr. Sybrandt says :

"Our subject was the topic used by the Christian Endeavor Society in the evening, and found in the eighth chapter of Romans.   (Rom. viii. 12–17, 31–39.)   I called attention to one verse in the chapter. 'For I reckon that the sufferings of this present life are not worthy to be compared with the glory that shall be revealed in us.' The last one to pray before myself was Robert Ross. . . .   He prayed that he might be guided to know and do his duty at the coming election."

That simple scene, in the light of subsequent events, becomes sublime.   It reminds us of the Ironsides of Cromwell preparing for battle by prayer.

His prayer was answered to the letter.   The reason for giving these facts, aside from their interest and historic value in illustration of the life of a hero and martyr, will appear in a later chapter.   It is easy to see that the society and its badge would naturally attract him.   It is not easy to see how any one could misconceive the facts, except through gross ignorance, stupidity, or malice, so as to endeavor to identify him with an alleged political-religious secret society, the " A. P. A.," or American Protective Association, now very much in evidence in all parts of the United States, and introduced again and again into the conditions that ended his life, and into the proceedings in court, in the trial of Bartholomew Shea as his murderer.

Pure and undefiled religion had the first place in the expression of Robert's nature and in the proportioning of his time and labors in behalf of the church. He was fond of amusements, of affording entertainment for others; but he did not reduce the church, as a means or an end, to the rank of a social club. He did not cease to cultivate himself, physically and mentally, when he withdrew from school into business; yet he did not transform the church into an evening school nor a parlor for society. He had the power and the taste for self-culture. He used his gifts freely and incessantly for the benefit of others. He was always losing his own life; but on the principle revealed and formulated by Jesus of Nazareth, he was finding it again in the lives of others. To say so is to narrate history, not to indulge in eulogy.

The ninth anniversary of the Young People's
Christian Union of his church occurred Sabbath
evening, November 25, 1891.   His elocutionary
gifts were utilized on that occasion in the recita-
tion of a sacred poem which had been published
in the *New York Observer.*   It was entitled

"THERE IS BUT ONE BOOK."

(From the last words of Sir Walter Scott.)

BY MRS. AGNES E. MITCHELL.

Fetch me the Buke, dear Lockhart,
An' gie me ane sweet ward.
What buke? there is nae ither, —
The Life o' th' Incarnate Lord;
I feel the shadows creepin' :
My licht's nae burnin' lang,
Sae read frae the blessit gospels
A bit, chiel, ere I gang ;
Fin' whaur He holpit the needy,
His pity wi' His micht ! —
Oh, my soul's fair hungry, Lockhart,
For the Livin' Bread, the nicht;

I think o' the dear disciples
Sae tassit on the sea,
An' the wards he spak' tae Simon, —
I ken they'd comfort me;
Tell o' the chitterin' sparrows, —
" Nae wan o' them can fa'; "

Tell hoo he callit the bairnies, —
The dearest thocht o' a';
Read owre hoo the ravin' tempest
Seekit silence i' the deep;
Sae the surges i' my bosom
Are croonin' a' tae sleep;

Ye maun catch the roll o' Jordan
I' his wards tae the Pharisee,
But ye'll hear him prayin', dearie,
I' the sough o' Galilee;
Dinna fash 'bout Judas's kisses;
Nae greet i' the garden dim,
But joy hoo the dyin' beggar
Foun' paradise wi' Him;
Nae hent o' Thamas dootin',
Nae ward hoo Peter fell;
It grie's me, sair, — their weakness
Wha ken't oor Lord sae weel;

Read o' the walk tae Emmaus
That long an' tearfu' day,
An' lat oor hearts burn, Lockhart,
As we gang the countrie way;
Pluck me ane lily, Lockhart,
A' siller-dewt an' sweet;
I speer the rose o' Sharon,
An' smell the growin' wheat;
Lat's join the throngin', dearie.
An' wait i' the wee bit ships
For the wards, like beads o' honey,
That fa' frae His haly lips;

Hoo sad the gospels, Lockhart,
Wi' His wand'rin', hameless life;
But there's ane grief fetches comfort,
Ane rest that comes o' strife;
Noo tak' me, kin' gude Lockhart, —
Aye tenner-true tae me ! —
Oot wi' the dear disciples,
" As far 's tae Bethany ; "
I sair need rest, belov'd,
An' the licht's a-wearin' dim;
But heaven's nae far frae Bethany,
An' sune I'll be wi' Him.

The selection is Scotch throughout. The re-
citer was of Scotch descent, and he rendered
effectively the sentiment by his power to inter-
pret the meaning through accurate and forcible
utterance of the dialect. It would be a difficult
task for a trained elocutionist who had not the
Scotch twist in his tongue.

When Robert was shot, he died without uttering
a word. If, like his brother William, he had been
wounded, and his sick chamber, unlike William's,
had become his death chamber, we can easily
imagine him uttering sentiments like those of the
last verse of the preceding poem. Bethany was a
hill-town. Troy is a hilly city. Ross's home was
on one of the hill-sides, and in reality heaven for

him was not far away. Like Enoch, he walked
with God, and in the midst of a deadly strife he
soon was not ; for not only the cowardly, brutal
assassin, but the all-controlling God took him.

Wednesday evening, October 25, 1893, an entertainment was given in the Oakwood Avenue
Presbyterian Church, to raise funds for sending
two delegates to the Council of the Brotherhood
of Andrew and Philip, in New York. It might
be called "The Society of the Innocents," so far
as itself or Robert Ross could be identified in any
way, good, bad, or indifferent, with the "A. P. A."
Or it might be called the two-letter society as distinct from the three-letter " A. P. A.," or the
several kindred four-letter societies, male and female, like the " Y. P. C. U.," the " Y. M. C. A.,"
the " W. C. T. U.," or the five-letter " Y. P. S. C.
E." Not one of the societies named, except the
" A. P. A.," is a secret society.

The subject of the entertainment was " The
White City " — the World's Fair in Chicago.
" Seven Oakwooders " told what they saw and
heard there, inclusive of the Ferris Wheel, the
Moorish palace, Russian carriages, the dairy and
stock-yard, agriculture, machinery, the battle-ship,

Lot's wife, the street of Cairo, the electric fountains, Buffalo Bill, humbugs, big valve, big tree,
and big telescope.

Robert had been one of the visitors and in-
vestigators, and was one of the select seven who
were to lecture and report in " Big Talks." His
subject was the " Electric Fountains," fascinating
to him as a master mechanic, and to all visitors and
listeners. He gave a very interesting explanation
of them. Sufficient money was raised for the
purpose in hand.

Such was Robert Ross, the alert, active boy ;
the agreeable, companionable youth ; the stalwart,
full-grown man ; the earnest, exemplary, influential,
loved, admired Christian ; a Timothy under the
tuition of his parents, and in association with a
minister of the gospel. His pastor never saw him
angry. He was at the opposite extreme from that
of the Pharisee. He identified religion and morality. He did not divorce them so as to make the
two contradictory to each other.

If American Christian homes, the public schools
and Sabbath-schools, and the varied Young Peo-
ples' Societies produce one like him occasionally,
they do well. If their united and co-operating

forces can multiply the number by ten, or one
hundred, or one hundred thousand, the advancement and regeneration of the nation will be accel-
erated at a rapid rate, and soon the final Kingdom
of God will be at hand.

CHAPTER IV.

MARTYRDOM AND TRANSFIGURATION.

THERE were events that preceded the fated election day of March 6, that were preludes to the revealed heroism of the several male members of the Ross family and to the shooting of one of them and to the martyrdom of Robert. February 3, 1894, a " revolver caucus " was held, so called because of the use of revolvers to accomplish election purposes through fraud and violence. It was held in the first election district, on the west side of River Street. Inside of the room was one John McGough, who claimed to be a Republican, manipulating votes. On the outside were Bartholomew Shea, Jerry Cleary, Owen Judge, and others of the same stamp. The caucus was Republican, but the men named were reputed Democrats. They had no moral right to be there, and such as they will have no legal right hereafter if proposed State laws fixing penalties for such conduct are enacted and executed. Democrats and residents in other wards voted. Repeaters voted. Pistol politics were exhibited in attempts to prostitute the purity of the ballot.

Stanley O'Keefe was at the caucus, but testified at the murder trial that he did not take an active part.

"Did you vote?" asked the counsel for the prosecution.

"Yes, sir," was the reply.

"Are you a Republican?"

"No, sir," replied the witness; and then, seeing his mistake, he said that in ward elections he was neutral.

John H. Boland, a well-known citizen and business man, an Irishman, a Roman Catholic, demanded that such voting should cease. John Ross was in the room. Turmoil ensued; the crowd from the outside forced its way into the room, and "Bat" Shea ran out the back way with the ballot-box, covering his retreat with a revolver.

When on the witness stand, he was asked, —

"What use did you have for the ballot-box?" and he answered, "None."

"What did you take it for?"

"For safe keeping."

" How many more ballots were in the box when you returned it to McGough than before you got it ? "

" I didn't count them."

The caucus related to the election of an alder-man.   The ballot-box was returned, the caucus continued, and McGough and his assistant declared their candidate the successful candidate.   Mean-while, the people opposed to the designers and repeaters, among whom were the Ross boys, held another caucus.

Their father was choked at the election in No-vember, 1893, by a policeman, when Robert was ejected from the polls for challenging illegal voters, and the other Ross boys were driven away.

The Rosses were determined, yet not defiant. Antagonism to themselves as citizens and Repub-licans was to be met by resistance, in the interests of a pure and protected ballot.   They knew their personal rights and the common rights of citizens, and dared to maintain them.   Hence they were hated.   Cowardice or courage was their alterna-tive, and they showed courage.   Submission or brigandage was the alternative of McGough and Shea, who were lawless and wicked enough to resort to further violence; to carry firearms, and, in madness or desperation, to discharge them with deadly aim and consequences. The next natural meeting and test of both sides would be at the election a month later. The Rosses knew that their lives were in danger, took legal counsel, secured cocobola sticks, ten and a half inches long, for defensive purposes, turned them at their own works, and distributed them among their co-workers, who were watchers of the polls. About a dozen of these sticks were distributed, but not all were actually carried to the polls. Robert Ross had one, but evidently lost it when he fell in the gully. One was used with good effect :

During the indiscriminate yet deadly firing of revolvers that occurred at noon, March 6, a revolver shot flashed in the face of Adam Ross, 2d. He turned, and saw a revolver pointed at his head. He threw up his hand and pushed up the revolver, and the weapon exploded over his head. He drew his stick from his inside pocket and struck his assailant, who fell. No further attention was paid to the fallen assailant, because Robert had been shot, and needed and received attention.

The legal counsel that the Rosses had received

was supported by the advice of Governor Flower, given to a committee of citizens who waited on him in Albany, on the day previous to election, that repeaters should be driven from the polls.

The polling-place on election day was a one-story frame house on the eastern side of Orr Street, in North Troy. It stands by itself in the picture of its surroundings. Across the street is a gully filled with brush, the whole scene being then bare of verdure, owing to the season of the year. On election morning law-abiding citizens who knew the bravado and criminality of the roughs with whom they were dealing were early at the polls, determined by their presence, their numbers, their character and reputation, to prevent illegal voting. The roughs were not over-awed. They too appeared, and carried concealed firearms, contrary to law. The Rosses did not carry firearms, even for defence. The watchers represented the Republican, Democratic, Socialist-Labor, and Prohibition parties. Neither McGough nor Shea were registered voters in the third district of the thirteenth ward. All the male members of the Ross family were registered voters in that ward and district. Between ten and eleven o'clock in

Polling Booth where Robert Ross was Killed.

the morning William Ross spoke to Martin Kane, a policeman who was off duty. As he did so, Shea reached over and struck him in the face. His younger brother John, diplomatic, but wise, said to him, "Take that; we don't want any trouble here."

Repeaters voted on four names; and the inspector of election at the trial of Shea testified that he knew all four persons, and that the men who voted were not those persons. They were compelled to swear in their votes. They entered the polling-place in a line. The Democratic inspectors did not challenge any voters. The name of William Armstrong was one of the names illegally voted on. He testified as follows, —

" I got my ballots and went into the booth. I was folding the ballots when I heard my name called out. I then stepped out of the booth and faced a man, whom I asked, 'Are you William Armstrong?'—'Yes, I am,' said he. 'Do you live at 53 Glen Avenue?' I asked. The man said he did; but I told him he did not, for I was the only William Armstrong who lived there. I told the election officers not to take the vote, and then stepped back into the booth and completed my ballots. When I went out to vote I was compelled to swear it in, some one having voted on my name."

Armstrong's vote was cast about half-past twelve o'clock. A fifth repeater, hearing the discharge of firearms on the outside, discontinued his attempt to vote, and escaped.

The firing had been occasioned by the fact that a protest had been made by Ellis Hayner, a representative watcher, against the illegal voting. Hayner was struck; William Ross was shot in the back of the head, and did not see who shot him ; Robert Ross was murdered. He was bareheaded when shot. His face was turned to the west. Bartholomew Shea fired the fatal shot, standing within two feet of him. Robert had fallen while pursuing McGough, the assailant of his brother. Four or five months previously, on his way from Long Island City, where he had been engaged in putting a motor in a church organ, to Brooklyn, he crossed Newtown Creek. He was in a great hurry to keep an appointment he had made ; and, without waiting until the draw in the bridge upon which he had stepped had swung to its place, he jumped to the other part of the bridge, and sprained his ankle. He was laid up for a couple of weeks, and his ankle was left so weak that when he stepped upon a small stone it would throw him down. It was still weak at the time of the tragedy. These facts probably account for his sinking to a sitting position. Shea took advantage of the situation, came close to him, and fired the fatal shot ; then escaped, and afterward was arrested. He passed between William and Robert Ross while firing. John Ross was quick to reach Robert and minister to him ; and he exclaimed, "If there are American citizens here, arrest that man !" meaning the fleeing murderer. One hundred people stood about the polls at the time of the tragedy.

The firing was general and rapid from the crowd of roughs, a fusillade "sounding like a bunch of fire-crackers." From fifteen to twenty shots are supposed to have been fired. It seemed, said one witness, as if a Wild West show were in progress. Shea himself received a scalp wound. It could not have been made by Robert Ross, for he had no revolver. He was abundantly able to defend himself in tackle with most men ; he was conscious of the fact, and he acted accordingly. Hatred was not in his heart, except the righteous anger against criminals and brutes, without which human nature is dehumanized and un-Christianized.

Dr. S. F. Rogers, M.D., who made the post-mortem examination, has made many similar examinations, but has never seen " a finer specimen of physical manhood than the dead man."

We have given the facts, not as derived from rumor, nor from newspapers only, nor from the family and friends, but from legal proceedings, the coroner's inquest, and the trial of the murderer. Excitement followed as a matter of course. The instincts of the people, true as truth itself, discerned instantly that Robert Ross was something more than a victim and an unfortunate; that he was not only blameless, but heroic and representative; that he had died for a principle, for the purity of elections, for an honest ballot in the voting and the counting, for the preservation of American institutions. He was a martyr, "a blessed martyr." His blood was sacrificial blood, and Providence would make it the seed of municipal purification and reform. He died on Tuesday.

The indignation meeting of Thursday evening was succeeded by the funeral on Friday afternoon. Twice, on successive days, the city paid its tribute of affection to its dead hero and its transfigured martyr.

Troy has known the pomp and glory of military funerals, in the burial of Major-General Wool (1788–1869), Colonel Ellsworth (1837–1861), and Major-General George H. Thomas (1816–1870). General Wool was a hero of the War of 1812, of the Mexican War, of Indian warfare, and of our Civil War. Troy honored him because in 1813 he had opened a recruiting office in what was then a village, and had circulated an appeal "to the patriotic young men of the counties of Rensselaer and Washington," urging them "to avenge the wrongs committed on our sacred country, or die in the attempt." Robert Ross believed that such an appeal had come to him from God, and he died in the attempt to prevent and undo the wrongs committed against his city and country.

Colonel Elmer Ellsworth, who was shot in 1861, at Alexandria, Va., while hauling down a Confederate flag, was a former Trojan, not by birth, but transient residence and engagement in business. Frank Brownell, his avenger, was a Trojan. Hence both men were highly honored in appropriate ways, as the remains of Ellsworth passed through Troy on their way to Mechanicsville, N.Y., for burial.

General George H. Thomas, "the Rock of Chickamauga," died in San Francisco in 1870, and his body was brought to Troy for burial in beautiful Oakwood Cemetery, closely following that of General Wool to its last resting-place.   President Grant and the members of his cabinet, Generals Sherman, Sheridan, and Meade, attended the funeral.

Troy has known, also, the solemnity and awe and righteous but suppressed wrath attending the burial of a leading citizen and public official who was murdered.   In 1867 Thomas H. Bailey, Chief Engineer of Hugh Ranken Steamer Company No. 2, was shot and killed without cause ; and his funeral occurred from the same Second Presbyterian church as the funeral of Robert Ross. Similarly, it was attended by crowds far too numerous to secure admission into the church.

It is with such men, and such mournful yet honoring and honorable conditions, that Robert Ross and his funeral and burial are to be classed ; yet from which his life and death are isolated and differentiated.   He was a private citizen, the youngest of those mentioned.   They were all heroes, and he was a hero.   Three were soldiers ;

but he was not a soldier. Two were firemen, and
he was a fireman. But, strictly speaking, he alone
was a martyr. His funeral was a civic funeral;
and Trojans, irrespective of sect, political party,
or social rank, were his mourners, save as his an-
tagonists at the polls had sympathizers among
men of their own class; and a few political parti-
sans sought to eliminate the thought of martyrdom, by representing the result as due to partisan
or religious strife, and a personal encounter between a few individuals and ward factions. Senator Murphy of the United States Senate, and a
resident of Troy, regarded the killing and death
as "deplorable." Less than that no one ought to
say who believes in law and order, in human freedom and righteousness.

The funeral addresses were delivered by the
Rev. Wm. H. Sybrandt and the Rev. James W.
Ford. The address of the pastor of the deceased,
the intimate friend of the living and the dead of
the family, was brief but comprehensive. It out-
lined Robert's youthful life, characterized him
worthily, and drew the lessons of his career as
teaching the manliness of true Christianity and
the nobility of blameless and zealous Christian

citizenship. The family requested that there be no police protection at the funeral. The request was granted, and there was good order, notwithstanding the vast crowds. Likewise, at their request, there was no band music. Doring's band had been engaged by the Republican club. The vocal and instrumental (organ) music was by the most gifted musicians of the city, members of the Mendelssohn quartet. Two brothers and four cousins of the deceased acted as pall-bearers. The Esek Bussey Fire Company, of which he was a member, was strongly represented at the funeral service and in the line of march. The Andrew and Philip Brotherhood wore their colors, red, orange, and black. The organ loft was draped with the American flag; the pulpit with mourning and patriotic emblems. The tolling of the church bell could be heard by the murderer confined in the Troy jail.

The burial was in Oakwood Cemetery; one of the most beautiful cemeteries in the country. It is not far from the scenes of the martyr's entire life. It commands extensive prospects of the surrounding country. It contains the Gardner Earl Memorial Chapel, a beautiful and imposing

Floral Tributes at the Grave of Robert Ross.

Romanesque structure, whose tower is as conspicuous as the cluster of towers on the Roman
Catholic Theological Seminary, and equally conspicuous in arresting the attention of travellers,
in entering or leaving the city.

The monument that contains the portrait of
Robert is a family monument owned by his father
and his uncle, Adam Ross. The flowers that
environ it tell their own story. The inscriptions
bespeak the love of his nearest kindred, and of
his youthful associates in the Brotherhood of
Andrew and Philip, and in social, business, and
religious life. Among them was a beautiful
wreath, bearing the familiar name " Rob " in im-
mortelles, sent by his intended bride. They tell
how " He Stood for His Rights," as a man and
an American. They record that he died as a
" martyr." The cross on which the Saviour died,
whose atonement he accepted, is repeatedly symbolized. The flag that he revered as the emblem
of his country is in the foreground and in the
background. The dove, emblem of the Spirit of
God, as the life of the spirit of man, and the generator of holiness in men, is pictured with great
beauty and reverence. The whiteness of his life

is symbolized by the entire collection of flowers and groups of designs. The wreath and the harp are suggestive of his condition and occupation in the regions of bliss and immortality. The grave of his sister Jennie, who, in 1887 and in her sixteenth year, died of slow fever, is concealed ; but they who were united to Christ in life, and who are asleep in Jesus, are reunited, we may be sure, where "there shall be no more death," no more sorrow, nor crying, nor pain.

The burial is not only in a beautiful cemetery and location, but in comparatively close neighborhood with two of the nation's great generals whom we have named. The monument to General Wool is the most conspicuous of the numerous monuments that adorn the city of the dead, and silently teach the lessons of the life that is life indeed. It consists of a stately monolith, seventy-five feet in height.

The inscription was composed by William Cullen Bryant, —

"THIS STONE IS ERECTED TO
MAJOR–GENERAL JOHN E. WOOL,
THE GALLANT SOLDIER,
THE ABLE COMMANDER, AND THE PATRIOTIC CITIZEN,
DISTINGUISHED IN MANY BATTLES."

The monument to General Thomas, in another part of the extensive grounds, is a finely sculptured sarcophagus, surmounted with a granite American eagle, grasping in its talons an accurate representation of the sword used by him and with which he obtained renown during the war.

A suitable monument appropriate in design will be erected to Robert Ross, probably not in the cemetery nor on the spot where he was killed. A tablet on an inscribed stone will be sufficient for the latter place. "The Robert Ross Memorial Association" of Troy ladies was organized in Music Hall, Monday, March 26, and is now rapidly collecting funds, securing designs, and site, and will ultimately dedicate a bronze statue.[1]

Seminary Park was selected by the association, but refused by a tie vote of the Park Commissioners. It is an eminently desirable place in the heart of the city. The monument would be only two blocks distant from the splendid Soldiers' and Sailors' Monument on Washington Square, which commemorates the record of the men of Rensselaer County, New York, who took part in the Civil War of 1861–65. Its naval

[1] See Note, page 86.

scene on one of the sides in the lower stone-work, in bronze bas-reliefs, represents an engagement between the floating batteries, "The Monitor" and "The Merrimac," because two Trojans, John A. Griswold and John F. Winslow, obtained for Capt. John F. Ericsson, the contract for the construction of "The Monitor," and with Cornelius S. Bushnell of New Haven assumed the heavy responsibility of securing the government against all loss of money, if the vessel should prove unserviceable or incomplete.

A monument to Mrs. Emma Willard, the principal of the famous Troy Female Seminary, is to be erected in Seminary Park. A monument to the Rev. N. S. S. Beman, D.D., a clergyman of national reputation, and for a generation a leader in the Presbyterian Church in the United States, ought to be erected there. One of the parks of the city is already named after him.

The court-house in which the murderer of Robert Ross was tried and convicted faces Seminary Park. There was poetic justice in securing the verdict on the eve of the Fourth of July ; for he was a martyr to the cause of human liberty. If the statue of Robert Ross should face toward

Troy Court House.

the court-house, in gratitude for the accomplish-
ment of the ends of justice, and in appeal for the
enforcement of all laws, especially those intended
to secure a pure ballot and to punish the violators
of the laws of the suffrage, the proprieties would
be suitably observed. But another location must
be chosen.

An appropriate conclusion of this narrative of
pathetic and tragic facts which redound to the
glory of Robert Ross, and the credit and discredit of Troy, is the following poem by John C.
Ball, published in *The Troy Times*, April 3, —

IN MEMORIAM — ROBERT ROSS.

BY JOHN C. BALL.

A HERO slain! His sacred ashes rest
Where Oakwood's silence urns the hallowed dead,
In beauty near Troy's high industrial walls.
Slain! Slain for what? Slain for fair Freedom's sake!
Sad kinship weeps, a city's heart is stirred
With deep emotion, a great commonwealth,
Ay, a nation for a martyred son
Trembles from centre to circumference,
And queries, Why, O God, this sacrifice?
A hundred years a nation! This freedom?
The freedom which our fathers bought with blood,
That all inheritors should be to life,
Liberty, and pursuit of happiness?
O Freedom, thy fair name is writ in blood!

To espouse thy beauty is to win thee,
By force of arms: and then to hold thee fast
From ravishment still costs the price of blood.
Freedom, fair goddess of the human heart!
Thou priceless gift the soul of man esteems —
E'en death with thee amid dread war's alarms
Is counted gain, for then no slavery is;
And yet, to live and own thee as a guest,
Perpetual 'neath each roof-tree in the land,
Each loyal heart desires.   For this brave Ross
Upon thine altar shed his loyal blood;
And men and women weep.
                              Hail, goddess fair!
Thy votaries rear upon thine altared hills
Their heart's memorial to the loyal brave
Who gave his fresh young life a sacrifice.
We raise no bleeding hecatomb, nor pyre
Of sacrificial flame to unknown gods;
But to the God of justice and of right,
To thee, fair goddess — thou his gift to man —
And to Robert Ross — a martyred freeman —
We give the tribute of our grateful hearts.

TROY, N.Y., March 26, 1894.

NOTE.

About ten well-known artists, several of whom are ladies, will sub-
mit models by the first Tuesday in October, and from these, one will be
selected.   The successful artist will secure the commission, while a prize
of $250 will be given for the second best design, and another of $150 for
the third best.

CHAPTER V.

COMMITTEE OF ONE HUNDRED FOR PUBLIC SAFETY.

BEFORE Robert Ross was buried, the citizens of Troy had assembled in mass meetings, to commemorate his death and to institute measures for the safety not only of the lives of other citizens, but the security and welfare of the city itself. More than one man had been shot. More than two men had been fired at. More than three men had been threatened. More than four were regarded as in danger of their lives. The friends of several clergymen accompanied them for a number of days, knowing more than the clergymen themselves how numerous were the threats made against them, and how base and rash were the roughs who threatened.

The citizens' meetings were held in the Second Presbyterian and Second Baptist Churches on Fifth Avenue. In reality they were one meeting, and the addresses were repeated. Hon. Martin

I. Townsend, ex-Congressman, the Gladstone of Troy, characterized it as the grandest meeting which had ever been held in Troy during his experience of fifty years. Probably there has been not a single meeting in the city, of great public moment, for half a century, that he has not attended and in which he has not borne a prominent part. He is still "the old man eloquent" and witty.

The fact that the meeting was held so promptly was significant, itself an evidence of the revival of the Trojan spirit of earlier and better days. Before Fort Sumter was fired on in 1861, as soon as some of the Southern States had passed ordinances of secession, a number of Trojans volunteered their services to preserve the Federal Union, January 2, 1861. They formed an infantry company January 11, '61, "in anticipation" of the necessities that might arise from a rupture in civil affairs ; and "The Freeman Cadets" was the first purposely organized body of local soldiery north of Mason and Dixon's line to take part in the war inaugurated several months later. Troy sent the second regiment of the State to the war ; and Capt. John W. Armitage's Company, on

Thursday, April 18, 1861, tendered its services to Governor Morgan, the first company offered to and accepted by the State under President Lincoln's call for troops made on the previous Monday.

The speakers were representative men, in the pulpit, at the bar, and in business. They avowed that henceforth by the process of rebellion against tyranny and corruption, citizens should be free from brutality, from the audaciously illegal and perjured voter, from one-man power centralized in a political boss, and from the horde of illiterate, cheap, and crafty officials who had become lodged in the various branches of the city government. The Rev. L. M. S. Haynes, D.D., pastor of the First Baptist Church, characterized Robert Ross as a martyr as follows, —

"Thirty-two years ago the ninth day of August next, I was standing at the head of my battery on a little hillock facing Cedar Mountain in the State of Virginia. By my side stood a brave boy of nineteen summers in charge of one of the guns. Without a moment's warning, in the height of the battle, a shell from the enemy's side struck the lad on the side of the head, tearing it nearly off, and he fell at my feet a martyr for the cause of human liberty ; and I declare to-night to you that

Robert Ross, a brave, Christian, industrious, be-
nevolent young man, was just as much a martyr
as Nelson Phillips."

With equal clearness it was discerned and
asserted that Shea was a representative man, —
the representative of corruption in politics, of
bossism and brutality, of the completed products
of the saloon. The ruling politician of the city
for a decade and a half has been Edward Murphy,
Jr., now Junior U. S. Senator of the State of
New York. He was alderman of Troy in 1865,
fire commissioner from 1874 to 1879, mayor from
1875 to 1882. He has been a brewer since 1867,
his establishment containing all the modern in-
ventions and conveniences for malting and brew-
ing ale and porter. His business has induced
him to foster the multiplication of saloons, to
increase the sale of liquors, to be identified with
the wholesale and retail liquor traffic. In politics,
he has pressed the button, and the saloon and the
police have done the rest. This will explain why
the Rev. Eben Halley, D.D., spoke as follows, —

"I have lived in Troy eight years, and I have
had young women come to me who were turned
out of their places as school-teachers ; and they

have said, ' Dr. Halley, what can you do for me ? ' and I have said, ' I can do nothing.' They have gone to the school commissioners, and they could do nothing ; but the school commissioners have said, 'You must go to the brewery ; ' and so we have found men who had influence at the brewery, and those teachers were retained in their positions. I have lived in this city, and I have seen it roll up a fraudulent majority. I have seen it roll up a fraudulent vote of three thousand five hundred, and you all know how that vote was secured."

At the conclusion of this meeting, a Committee of One Hundred for Public Safety was appointed. It was composed of representatives of the religion, the culture, the business, the enterprise, of the city, and of opposing faiths in religion and politics. Hence it was non-partisan. Partisanship under such conditions as then prevailed is treason.

The Rev. Theophilus P. Sawin, pastor of the First Presbyterian Church, in addressing the meeting of the ladies in Music Hall, where the "Robert Ross Monument Association " originated, said, " On this issue (legal and pure elections) all honest men are Catholic in their desire for universal right, and all are Protestant in their warfare against wrong."

Senator Murphy was not appointed on the committee, but his parish priest, the Rev. Peter Havermans, was appointed. Father Havermans is to the Roman Catholicism of Troy what Hon. Martin I. Townsend has been to its civic life. He is nearly ninety years of age. He was the second Roman Catholic priest in the United States to manifest his own loyalty and that of his parishioners, in 1861, by hoisting a United States flag on the steeple of St. Mary's Church, and he kept it floating there until the close of the war. He has freely fraternized with Protestants.

Ex-Director of the Rensselaer Polytechnic Institute, David M. Greene, Civil Engineer, has been the chairman of the committee. Its meetings have been secret and its proceedings confidential. Its work, in part, has consisted in aiding the legal prosecution of the murderer of Robert Ross, associating itself with the municipal reform movement throughout the State and the nation through the Municipal and Lyceum Leagues, the City and Civic and Good Government Clubs. The committee was represented in the national organization that was formed in New York City, May 28 and 29. A large delegation of the committee visited New York, April 18, by special invitation, and two of its legal members, Seymour Van Santvoord and George B. Wellington, addressed the City and Good Government Clubs. Attorney Wellington spoke as follows of election methods in Troy : —

"For fifteen years, at least, there has not been an honest election in the city of Troy — city, county, State, or national. Within a circle, of which Troy might be considered a centre, with a radius of nine miles, there has been a number of elections in which enough fraudulent votes were cast to change the election of a president of the United States, and State officials in every department of our State service, not excluding the judiciary. The nature of the crimes committed you know, but I will enumerate them : Voting on names of persons not electors within the district ; repeating, i.e., voting on the names of electors a number of times ; stuffing ballot boxes ; stealing ballot boxes and substituting others with ballots therein not cast ; false counting ; falsifying the returns ; and bribery. Repeating, technically so-called, is of comparatively recent origin, . . . that is, voting twice, thrice, four times on a single name. . . . In some districts last fall the votes of repeaters, demonstrably such, were equal to at least twenty-five per cent of the lawful vote cast. . . . Every attempt to correct the evil has met with vigorous opposi-

tion.   There is an organization in Troy which sup-
ports with its influence and its money this evil.
. . .   Repeaters are given names to vote on and
are told the residences they are to claim.   Who
instructs them?   There is a common aim among a
miserable lot of criminals of low intellectual order,
scattered through a city strange to many of them,
to violate the law, which they do without hin-
drance.   They are paid for their work.   They
have their guides and instructors.   The guides
act with a common design. . . .   It is the guilt
of bribery that has made cowards of many of our
citizens and has made criminally inefficient many
of our officials.

"The power which has ruled us has controlled
absolutely every department of our city and county
government.   During all the years that have been
filled with open, boastful crimes against our liberties, not a single conviction was ever had in our
county for an offence against the ballot until this
spring, when one man pleaded guilty to an indictment for false voting, and was sent to the
penitentiary.   During that period not a single
indictment was ever found for election crimes
until this spring, when two indictments were found
out of over thirty cases, which were in every respect complete.   Indeed, it became impossible to
get a grand jury drawn according to the statute."

The charge of bribery is serious enough ; but it
is not the most serious charge that has been made

against "the powers that be" in Troy, and of whom it can hardly be said with truth, that they are ordained of God. During the trial of the murderer of Robert Ross, the charge of conspiracy was made by the prosecution, conspiracy between politicians and roughs, against the lives of the watchers of the polls in the 13th ward on election day.

Mrs. Thomas A. Titus testified that on that day she stood near a barn on Douw Street, not far from the polling-place, and heard a conversation while she stood there.

Six persons were together in a group, one man standing against the barn and the other five surrounded him. Mrs. Titus testified as follows : —

"I stood six feet away from them with my back turned. Two of the six men were Shea and McGough. . I heard the men say, 'We'll slug them.' 'Kill them, and twenty-five dollars is yours!'

"Then I heard a man say, 'Well, slug them and kill them if you can, and twenty-five dollars is yours.' I heard one of the men say, 'How do I know I'll get my money?' To this the man who stood against the barn answered, 'Your money will be waiting for you when the work is done.' The men then went over in the direction of the polling-place."

The deliberation with which Shea shot Ross was terrible; but here is evidence that seems to be proof, that he did it for a price, and a small one. The assistant-district attorney compared him to Judas, who not only betrayed Jesus, but did it for thirty pieces of silver.

The Committee of Public Safety prepared a bill which was passed by the State legislature, that legislated out of office the entire Troy police force — commissioners, chief, captains, sergeants, detectives, and patrolmen ! No person who had not been a citizen of the United States five years was to be eligible to appointment on the force, or who had ever been convicted of crime, or who could not read and write the English language understandingly. A clause provided that it should be the duty of every member of the force to arrest repeaters on election day without a warrant, and that at least five days prior to every election the superintendent should issue an order so instructing the officers.

While it was in charge of Governor Flower, for his signature or veto, the committee delivered to him, Monday, April 23, a communication, urging him to sign it, on the ground of the inefficiency of

Judge Williams, who sentenced the Murderer of Robert Ross.

Published in the Troy Times. Reproduced by permission.

the police and the insecurity of life and property under their charge.

The following illustrations of inefficiency and insecurity were given, inclusive of direct reference to issues and conditions resulting from the death of Robert Ross : —

"(1.) On April 19, about four o'clock in the afternoon, in a place of business on Fourth Street, within two blocks of police headquarters, near the heart of the city, a reputable merchant was shot down in his office by two thieves, who entered and attempted to rob the safe. After the shooting the thieves passed into the street and escaped. In their flight through the city they traversed a distance of over a mile, and were pursued by a large concourse of people ; but not a policeman was seen in the entire course of the flight. The thieves were armed, and at intervals fired at their pursuers. Their victim died the following morning, but the criminals have not yet been arrested.

"(2.) On the 16th of the month a man named Lee, employed in a collar manufactory on River Street, the main thoroughfare of Troy, was standing in the doorway of the factory, in broad daylight. He was fired at by two men, who, after shooting, drove away. The intended victim was not hit, but the bullet lodged near him in the casing of the door. No arrests have been made.

Mr. Lee was a witness against Shea at the Ross inquest.

"(3.) On Wednesday evening of this week, about half-past nine, a woman was assaulted on Pawling Avenue, one of the principal suburban streets. She was thrown down and her clothing was torn, but her assailant was driven away by a citizen who was passing. No arrest has been made in this case.

"(4.) A few days ago a respectable citizen of the thirteenth ward, passing to his home late in the evening, was intercepted and pursued by ruffians, and was obliged to take refuge in the house of a neighbor, and remained there all night. This gentleman was also a witness against Shea at the Ross inquest.

" The above occurrences have all taken place within ten days, in the most populous and frequented sections of the city. All the criminals are at large."

Governor Flower vetoed the bill, partly on account of his own " supposition " that the bill was not wanted by a majority of the people of Troy. An interesting cartoon relating to himself and Senator Murphy was published in *Judge*, March 24, and an equally suggestive one relating to the Senator and Shea in *Frank Leslie's Illustrated Weekly*, March 22, entitled " Victim, Culprit, Criminal."

CHAPTER VI.

UNDER THE STARS AND STRIPES.

FIVE times the name of Ross has been prominent in the history of this nation. First
came Mrs. John Ross, familiarly known as
" Betsy," who, with the co-operation of Gen.
George Washington, made the first American
flag ; next Colonel George Ross, who signed the
Declaration of Independence ; then in the War of
1812, General Robert Ross; then Charlie Ross,
the lost boy ; and then Robert Ross of Troy, the
Martyr ! Attention was called to the facts at the
funeral of Robert Ross, by the Rev. Wm. H.
Sybrandt. Three times out of the five the name
has appeared conspicuously as the name of patriots, — colonial, national, and municipal patriots.
"Betsy" Ross contributed her skill, her ingenuity, her superior taste, her poetic and vocal
powers, her loyal enthusiasm, to the welfare of
the country. She was the most artistic uphol-
steress in the land in the period covered by the

struggle for American Independence, using the best quality of silks and satins, and originating designs that were proofs of the possession of artistic taste and ability. She was a Friend, or Quaker, residing in Philadelphia, a city conspicuous in the entire history of the period. She made and partially designed the stars and stripes, the first star-spangled banner that ever floated on the breeze. The house in which she did the work is still standing, No. 239 Arch Street, a little two-story attic tenement, first occupied by Mrs. Ross after she became a widow.

Colonel George Ross, her brother-in-law, a member of the Continental Congress and a signer of the Declaration of Independence, was a member of a Congressional committee that in June, 1776, accompanied by General George Washington, called upon her, and engaged her to make the flag from a rough drawing, which, according to her suggestions, was redrawn by Washington with pen and pencil, then and there, in her modest back parlor. The flag as there designed was adopted by Congress. Mrs. Ross became flag-maker for the government, and continued the work for more than fifty-five years. There is on record an order on the treasury department "to pay Betsy Ross fourteen pounds twelve shillings and threepence for flags for the fleet in the Delaware River."

Her daughters succeeded to the work, and became known as the most patriotic ladies in the land. Our country had no name until she marked upon her flags, " The United States of America." Quaker as she was, she refused to be silent, and she exclaimed, " My voice shall be devoted to God and my country, and whenever the Spirit moves me, I'll sing and shout for liberty." She sang to the volunteers her own " War Song for Independence."

The red stripes in the design for The Flag were emblematic of fervency and zeal; the white of integrity and purity; the blue field, with stars, of unity, power, and glory. They might be construed as typical of the patriotic record and personal character of those members of the Ross family that have lived, suffered, or died for their country. The beauty and sentiment of the artistic woman, inwrought into the design and colors of the flag, have been a vital power in inspiring patriotic sentiment from the very origin of American Independence until now.

Colonel George Ross, born in Delaware, served without pay in the colonial legislature of Pennsylvania, co-operated with William Penn in behalf of the Indians, was a member of Congress and a signer of the Declaration of Independence. One historian says that in every leading measure in favor of freedom he was a leading man.

At Bladenburg, Md., in 1814, General Robert Ross, commanding four thousand veterans of the British army, encountered Gen. William H. Winder. He landed his troops below the city, and commenced marching on it, while the British fleet prepared for the bombardment of Fort Mc-Henry. From the fort a little vessel came gliding down the bay, bearing a flag of truce, and heading for the flagship of the British squadron. It was guided by Francis Scott Key, going to intercede for a friend who had been taken prisoner. He was detained, saw the bombardment of the fort, September 13, 14; and when he saw the flag survive the bombardment, was impelled to write what proved to be a national song, "The Star Spangled Banner."

What's in a name? What a contrast between the British Robert Ross, the soldier of 1814, and the young American Robert Ross, the civilian of 1894, exactly threescore years later! The one fired on the American flag, and if possible would have been shot on the spot. The other appropriated it as the dearest symbol of love of country, with which his heart was full.

There is no need of mentioning further the name of Charlie Ross, except to note that he too was a Philadelphian, like his ancestral namesakes and remote relatives, a child of the very home of early patriotism, next to the capital of the nation.

Robert Ross had ordered several dozens of the national flag, to be used by himself and his associate watchers on election day; but these unfortunately did not arrive until after he was shot, or he would have died decorated with the national colors. His solitary act recalls the early days of the war, when, because the flag had been hauled down at Sumter, it went up in Northern cities, towns, and villages, and women wore miniature banners on their bonnets, and men carried emblems in breastpins and countless other devices.

The martyrdom itself, and the nobly sentimen-

tal use and inspiration of "Old Glory," quickly
induced Presbyterian pastors and Sabbath-schools
in Troy to decorate their Sabbath-school rooms
permanently with the national colors. Before
the month of March was concluded, two flags
were presented to the Westminster Presbyterian
Sabbath-school in Troy, as permanent ornamental features of the school, and as an inspiration
to youthful religious patriotism. The pastor of
the church, Rev. George Fairlee, had suggested
such a general movement in a sermon, and his
own people adopted it within two weeks.

Similar events occurred in the Woodside Presbyterian Church and Sabbath-school in South Troy,
of which the Rev. Arthur Allen is pastor. It is
located at the opposite extreme of the city from
the Oakwood or Westminster churches. In an
editorial on the local situation, the *Troy Times* of
March 26, 1894, said, —

"The American flag should be in every Sunday-
school in the United States, and wave over every
schoolhouse."

The Kingdom, a Congregational weekly, published in Minneapolis, accepted the suggestion,

Residence of the Ross Family.

and in its issue for May 11 added the following comment : —

"In these days, when new emphasis is being placed upon the duties of citizenship, it is well that the religious instruction of the young should have incorporated with it teaching along these lines. There is no more suggestive symbol than the flag of our country."

Robert Ross will not lack for local memorials, and there is no disposition anywhere to force his name upon the country. But his death and its significance were commented upon by the press in all sections of the land. The local papers re-published extracts daily for weeks in succession, taken from the dailies and weeklies, the secular and religious press. Therefore national attention was arrested. What national memorial of the martyr could there be more fitting than a perennial education in patriotism under the folds of the flag of our Union and the inspirations of Ross's noble life and heroic death ? The flag is becoming more and more familiar in the public schools. Why not in the Sabbath-schools ? If an ideal inspiration and origin were to be sought for to initiate a movement for the universal use in

Sabbath-school rooms and services of the flag of the United States, could a better one be conceived or found than such a death of such a youth?

It is not proposed that there be the simultaneous observance of a given day in this connection. The movement simply proposes a method which will give rise to multiplied occasions for awakening love of country. If adopted, it will be a parallel movement with the one which honors the flag in the day-school. It will keep our national colors "flying" before thousands, even millions, of children seven days in the week and three hundred and sixty-five days in the year. If sentiment is worth anything, the chronic expression of it is worth everything. If youth is idealistic, the idealizing of our country and our flag cannot fail to be wholesome and abiding. Local patriotism, broadening into a love of home, of native or adopted city, of native or adopted state and country, is precisely the species of patriotism desired.

How shall the movement be inaugurated? Spontaneously, as it was in Troy, in Westminster Presbyterian Church and Sabbath-school. Parents can easily stimulate it. Let generous individuals and alert officials foster it. Youth themselves can promote it, for a creditable silk flag is not very expensive. When the flag is available, hail its advent with brief and pointed addresses on such themes as patriotism, obedience, fidelity, loyalty, courage, and Christian warfare, and with a rich programme of patriotic hymns. The story of the life and death of Robert Ross on such occasions will be worthy of narration and repetition. The 117th anniversary of the adoption of the Stars and Stripes, June 14, 1894, occurred while the Court of Oyer and Terminer, Justice Pardon C. Williams presiding, was engaged in securing a jury for the trial of his indicted murderer. The day occurs close to June 17, which is a legal holiday in Boston, observed in commemoration of the Battle of Bunker Hill.

The family of George Ross have been grateful for the honors paid to their deceased member. Their grief has had a modicum of joy that they were not called upon to bury more than one of their number; for three of the sons and brothers were fired at. William was shot behind the right ear, and the ball, taking a downward course, lodged in the neck, where it remains.

In consequence of the wound, his hearing on that side is somewhat impaired. Adam Ross, 2d, narrowly escaped. John was exposed to the indiscriminate firing. While confined to his sickroom on the day after Robert's funeral, William was interviewed by a reporter of *The Troy Times*, and informed that a monument to Robert had been proposed. His noble reply was, " The only monument we desire for our brother is the promise of a pure ballot in Troy." The words came slowly and earnestly, and were spoken from the brave man's heart.

The sentence is worthy of inscription on the monument to be erected.

CHAPTER VII.

FRIENDS AND FOES TO AMERICA.

THE biography of Robert Ross, from begin-
ning to end, deals with two groups of young
men. Both groups are typical. Both reveal the
well-known yet insufficiently emphasized fact, that
mankind are saved and rescued, or lost and ruined,
within the first third of the allotted threescore
years and ten. The records of church membership and of the State prison are in evidence on
this point. There are exceptions; but they are
not so numerous nor significant as to disprove
the rule. William Ross is the eldest of the four
brothers, and he is thirty-seven years of age;
John Ross is thirty-three; Adam Ross, 2d, is
thirty; Robert was twenty-five years and six
months old at the time of his death.

Bartholomew Shea is twenty-three years of
age; John McGough, who is under indictment for
the shooting of William Ross, is twenty-three;
Stanley O'Keefe, one of the principal witnesses

for the defence, is twenty-two ; Michael Delaney, another witness for the defence, is twenty-five.

The evidence given in court by their opponents themselves disclosed a heritage, a class of lives, and an environment directly opposed to the same species of facts in the lives of the assailed, wounded, and murdered Rosses. If the Rosses deserve to be commended, their opponents, of necessity, must be condemned, yet not without an expression of pity for them, and of hope for their social improvement and moral reform, in prison or out of it. They are human; they are neighbors in the Biblical and Christian sense ; they are to be visited, wherever they are, if they receive their dues, by representatives of Christ and the church. But their own testimony, publicly and legally given, has been that they have led the lives of idlers and thieves; that they have made the saloon, not the home nor the church, the centre of their career; and that they have been convicted of crimes. John McGough, while giving his testimony, was profane, and was rebuked by the examining counsel for the defence. He had been in the Reformatory, Elmira, N.Y., thirteen months, sentenced for burglary under a

plea of guilt. Stanley O'Keefe admitted that,
from October, 1893, until June, 1894, his occupation had been roaming around, and his headquarters had been on the streets ; that from March 6,
until June 30, 1894, or from the day of the election murder until the day of his testimony in
court, there had been "about six days " in which
he had not visited a particular saloon ; and that
within that period one of his companions had
worked only twelve or fifteen days. He himself
had served a sentence for three months in the
Albany penitentiary. Michael Delaney admitted
that he was a visitor at a given saloon six days
out of seven, and that he had lied to the jailer, in
order to secure an interview with his associate,
the murderer of Robert Ross. He was characterized by the counsel for the prosecution as "the
very opposite, in every respect, of the members
of the Committee for Public Safety." A majority
of this gang of roughs confessed that they were
accustomed to carry revolvers, buying or borrow-
ing, to suit their necessities and convenience.
Shea's revolver was admitted in evidence, show-
ing three discharged and three loaded cartridges.
Shea visited two saloons on election morning be-

fore the strife occurred at the polls. He acknowledged that he had lied to the superintendent of
police, to avoid incriminating himself, and that
he had assaulted a citizen in a street fight. Attorney George Raines, in summing up for the
prosecution, before the jury, said, —

"They are persons upon whose honor you
would not stake five dollars as a loan ; you would
not accept their word for the price of a ham ; you
would not leave your pocketbook in a saloon or
grocery store in the presence of any of them and
go away from it. You would not walk the streets
of Troy in company with any one of them. You
would not leave them in your house 'unattended'
with valuables exposed. . . . Not one of this
gang, either from sentiment or human pity or
from curiosity, gathered to the side of the dead
man on the dump across the street."

Representatives of the "gang" were constantly
in attendance as spectators in the court-room.
Their presence was observed by Judge Williams.
He called up the clerk for issuing subpœnas without authority, allowing his own friends to get into
court. The judge censured the coroner for quibbling about identifying property that had passed
through his hands. He reproved Attorney Hitt,

of the defence, for being too severe with a witness, — and all this in one afternoon.

The photographs of Bartholomew Shea and
John McGough, in contrast with those of the
Ross brothers, tell their own story of heredity
and viciousness ; but we do not care to present
them.

The saloon, therefore, on the testimony of such
witnesses, is their congenial haunt.

In a sermon delivered by the Rev. S. L. M.
Haynes of Troy, on the first Sabbath in June,
1894, in recognition of the semi-centennial of the
Y. M. C. A., he estimated that there were six
thousand young men in the city between fifteen
and thirty years of age. He said, —

"There are fifty churches in this city ; and if the
number of young men is the same in the other
churches as the number who attend this church,
we will have 1,000 young men in church and 5,000
not attending church. There are 800 saloons in
Troy, and about 8,000 men are in these saloons
every night."

Edward Murphy, Jr., brewer, makes his living,
secures his income, in co-operation with saloons,
aside from other sources of income and more

legitimate investments. The sale of the products
of the brewery is his principal business. He
and his find common ground in the saloon. The
saloon becomes a *political institution*, a political
retreat, a political centre, a political power for
base men and bad politics. Nothing good comes
from it, in the interests of the home or the church.
But this is not the point now emphasized. Nothing good issues from it, to promote the welfare of
the citizen, the voter, the municipality, the State,
the nation. Immorality and vice dwell in it.
Crimes against persons and property, against God
and man and the State, originate in it. It abides
as headquarters for criminals. Confessed criminals certify to the general facts, who are to be believed in this line of testimony, when they are
not to be believed in any other. The whole truth
was known before they testified.· It had been a
moral certainty. But it was legally proved. No
attempt was made to prove the connection between
the chief politician and his tools. But that there
is a direct connection between the set of politicians who will buy and force their way into office,
for the sake of further political advancement and
a partnership in the (financial) spoils, is not to be

doubted. Editor John A. Sleicher, of the New York Mail and Express, is a former Trojan, who has had a varied editorial experience in Troy, as well as in Albany and New York. While the trial of Shea, the man-slayer, was in progress, Mr. Sleicher made an address in New York, in which he evidently drew upon his knowledge gained as an editor in the cities named. He said that, —

"Boss rule means the seizure of municipal control by selfish and illiterate men, whose main support comes from the saloons, the gamblers and the haunts of vice. These latter find a profit in the partnership with politics ; and a part of the profit is the protection this partnership assures. It means the promotion of the ignorant and vicious, or of their servile tools, to places of power, to preside in our courts, to manage our public institutions, to clean our streets, conduct our schools, supervise our charities, and guard our peace. It means the sudden accumulation of enormous fortunes by men who look upon official station as a personal perquisite and on public office as a private snap.

"Three conditions are needed to secure municipal reform : First, honest elections ; secondly, a general awakening of civic pride among the masses ; and thirdly, united effort on the part of all good citizens."

The situation in Troy may be discerned in the light of a contrasting situation. Within a few days after the publication of the article in *The Golden Rule*, on the martyrdom of Robert Ross, by his present biographer, a letter was received from Grinnell, Iowa, in which the writer of it said that political bosses were unknown there, as they exist in Chicago, New York, and similar cities. Likewise stuffing of the ballot-boxes and repeating were unknown.

"No man here," said the correspondent, "black or white, rich or poor, ignorant or otherwise, is hindered in the least from going to the polls on election day, and quietly casting his ballot for whom he pleases, if by the law of the State he is entitled to a vote."

He referred to Grinnell, which is one of the oldest towns in Central Iowa, a college town that has never known the presence of a saloon, "a typical, if indeed not a model, temperance town." But he added : —

"I have never heard of any of these base practices before spoken of, in our inland temperance State capital, Des Moines, which is only seventy miles from here. I have been there, and have

friends living there also. Des Moines has been a
prohibition town at least for the last eight years,
during which time the outrages and frauds and
crimes have been holding sway in other places on
election days."

Iowa is in the main an agricultural State. The
situation in New York State, in the smaller cities
and in the rural districts, is a great contrast
to the condition in New York City, and in the
cities of mixed nationalities like Brooklyn, Troy,
and Buffalo. The license system, as related to
the saloon, prevails in the State. The system is
low in morals, even when it is *high* in law. The
boss is not universal, although the few great
bosses are all controlling. Nevertheless, it is
easy to see that Robert Ross in his boyhood,
in rural and prohibitory Iowa, prohibitory in sentiment before prohibitory in law, had seen a state
of things which in his young manhood made the
election conditions in Troy unendurable. He
must antagonize it in all possible ways, and he
did.

It is apparent that the political *boss* might "*go*"
and political corruption remain. Not until the
saloon is prohibited by law, and the law is en-

forced, will municipal reform be complete, even if
much progress is made through " an awakening of
civic pride," and " united effort on the part of all
good citizens." The principle of prohibition is to
be maintained, in the slow process of educating
and uneducating the people ; for they need not
only to advance to a discernment and assertion
of absolute righteousness in a matter of right and
wrong, but they need to outgrow and abandon
the policies and the so-called science of alcoholic
liquors, which have prevailed in this land from its
origin until now, and in the Old World from time
immemorial. There is a new science, and a better, because a truer one, which affirms that alcohol
is a poison, not a food. This is the science now
written in the text-books of the public schools,
whether taught by the teacher or not. It has the
indorsement of public, legal adoption. There is a
new legal procedure against the liquor traffic,
" not yet fifty years old," which in State Constitu-
tions, and in the statutes of States and cities,
prohibits the wholesale and retail traffic. The
historic attitude of the world and of this country
is to be changed and reversed. Biblical prophecy
predicts that the time will come when nations

will be born "at once." The signs of those times
do not appear as yet, the signs of immediate religious or moral regeneration. Unless the end
shall come suddenly, without foreshadowings,
they are far off, they are not at hand. But evidence is here presented that a determined few, a
small minority, a Gideon's band, may accomplish
much to secure a pure and honest ballot in the
cast and in the count, or to advance any reform.
One may chase a thousand, and two put ten thousand to flight. When the unexpected happens,
and a modern Cain slays a modern Abel, the
event is providentially permitted, so as to give an
emphasis not to be given in any other way to
the truth that the blood of the martyr is the seed
of the church. "He, being dead, yet speaketh."
The name of Robert Ross is the name to conjure
with in Troy to-day, in opposing the saloons, in
seeking a better observance of the Sabbath, in
the instruction of the young in the home and in
the schools, in issuing warnings against evil, and
the institutions that generate evil. His monument will speak "For God and Our Country"
through coming generations. The same vicious
elements that fought and shot him have threat-

ened to prevent the erection of the monument, and
to disfigure or destroy it if erected. But the threats
are made in a cowardly way, "anonymously," and
they are not feared nor overestimated. Henceforth, some laws against law-breakers will be enforced in Troy, the processes of law being initiated
and forwarded by the Committee of One Hundred
for Public Safety. Counsellor Raines, in his able,
eloquent, and scholarly address to the jury that
convicted the murderer, said, —

" To-morrow will be the anniversary of the sign-
ing of the Declaration of Independence. And
you, gentlemen, will be engaged in deciding anew
the great principles which that day exemplifies ;
in deciding whether or not republican institutions
shall stand, and whether government of organized
society shall continue to exist. The grand right
of a free people is the ballot. It was in the defence of that right that the young man who sleeps
under yonder hillside lost his life ; and it was in
opposition to this right that the power of organized evil strode into the place of the election to
eradicate whatever of security had been walled
up about the ballot, by the use of deadly weapons,
to accomplish a result not in accordance with the
majority in that district. . . . The question to
be decided at this bar of justice is not a question between the prosecution and defendant ; it is

Hon. George Raines.

Published in the Troy Times. Reproduced by permission.

the question between organized society and its
enemy. . . . You must decide whether or not
the assizes of the people for a trial by jury shall
be interrupted and dismissed by the crack of a
revolver. . . . The .American people are to-day
centering their attention upon the ballot — its
defence and protection. . . . If assassination is
to take its place in the politics of the American
people, and an American jury is to palliate such
an offence, a long stride will be taken in the direction of breaking down American institutions. . . .
These Trojans represented the culmination of the
character, manhood, and patriotism of our American people. . . . As to this matter of repeating,
I will say it is not a matter of one party or
another. You know these men are the hired
thugs of either party, or, I may say, of any party
who desires to hire them. With them it is a
matter of total indifference as to who is successful ; they go to the polls for pay, and they are for
whomsoever they can get to pay. They are a
menace to good citizenship ; and when the good
citizen stands in defence of the ballot-box, he
should be protected. It is a worthy cause to
engage in. So it was with Robert Ross. He
simply stood there as one protecting the honesty
and purity of the ballot, and he fought manfully
for the cause of right and good citizenship. Had
he gone away, had he fled, Robert Ross to-day
would still be walking the earth, a joy and comfort to his family and friends, but to himself
simply six feet three of undeserved and worthless

humanity to his mind and the dignity of his young
manhood.   But he had a high duty which he regarded, and which had to be performed.   He
stood fast at his post. . . .   Realize that it was
at the doorway of the sanctuary of American
liberty that this man fell ; and, as you see him
fall, realize that it devolves upon you to protect
each polling-place in the city of Troy and in the
State of New York and in the United States from
a repetition of that offence by which this fellow
lost his life."

CHAPTER VIII.

A. P. A. IN CONTROVERSY AND IN COURT.

A SECRET society, which was characterized in the trial of the murderer of Robert Ross as the American Protective Association, the American Protestant Association, and the American Proscriptive Association, figured prominently in his personal history during January and February, 1894, and in the subsequent history of his murderer. It has become known to the public as the "A. P. A." Neither Robert Ross nor his father nor any of his brothers were members of it ; yet persistent attempts have been made to identify them with it, and for the purpose of fastening upon them a charge of bigotry and intolerance.

January 14, F. Cops, a member of the Esek Bussey Steam and Fire Engine Company No. 8, published a list of fourteen names of members of that company as belonging to the "A. P. A." Among them were the names of Adam Ross, 2d, and John and Robert Ross.

The company held a special meeting February 5, and expelled the offending member, after he had admitted before the whole company that he had published the names out of spite, because he was a defeated candidate for office.

As soon as Robert Ross had been shot, and public indignation asserted itself, the prisoners arrested and confined for his murder and for shooting William, undertook to account for the tragedy by attributing it not to political but religious feeling. They issued a statement, March 10, which was published in one of the local papers March 11, alleging that the thirteenth ward was " a hotbed of bigotry and evil ; " and that those in that ward wha claimed to be loyal Americans were " not loyal Americans, but loyal A. P. A's., in heart, if not in organization." Such was their excuse or defence for carrying and using firearms, resorting to personal violence, murdering and attempting to murder. Their pronunciamento scarcely needs serious attention ; for even if all that they alleged was true, it could not be legitimately offered in court or in morals as a defence for depriving American citizens and voters of " life, liberty, and the pursuit of happiness." When the trial came, their counsel used all the resources of law to prevent confessed members of the " A. P. A." from being on the jury, on the ground of alleged prejudice against a " Roman Catholic " who was to be tried for his life. No member of the jury was a member of the " A. P. A." The last man accepted, Matthew Book, a farmer, was an avowed Catholic ; and he voted to convict, because the jury was unanimous as required by law, and the verdict was speedily reached after submission. The counsel for the defence, in his address to the jury, shifted the case from the religious to the political extreme, affirming that " it was conceived in politics, nurtured in politics, and politics had entered into it at every step."

" Did you not form any opinion as to whether any repeating was being perpetrated in the thirteenth ward ? " was a question asked of a juror by the counsel for the prosecution.

" I thought there was some political squabbling going on."

" Do you call shooting with pistols political squabbling ? " inquired the attorney, with thunder in his voice ; and then, as the juror hesitated, continued, " Do you call killing men political squabbling ? Is that fair game in Troy ? "

The witness was decidedly discomfited at this unexpected question, and tried to recede from the answer he had given.   He finally said that he considered it murder.

Undoubtedly the issues were political, in the best sense of the word.   The people were struggling for securing and maintaining their rights, and demanding a fair legal vote and an honest count.   Party and partisanship had been sacrificed for the sake of obtaining a pure and uncorrupted ballot.   All the Rosses were Republicans, but they were all working for the election of a Democratic mayor ; they were Scotch, yet were working for the election of an Irish Roman Catholic mayor. Such was their species of bigotry, or of race prejudice !   The issue hinged on the election of a mayor.   Both nominees were Democrats and Catholics.   Republicans made no nomination.

During the process of selecting the jury, some legal decisions were re-affirmed relating to all secret societies ; and some dialogues occurred between jurymen and counsel, of great interest alike to those who are and those who are not members of the " A. P. A."   The Court excused those who refused to say whether they

Jury before whom the Murderer of Robert Ross was Tried.

Published in the Troy Times. Reproduced by permission.

did or did not belong to the organization in question, whether designated in full or by initial letters ; not because they were disqualified by actual membership in it, but for reasons of expediency.

"This is an anti-Catholic organization, is it not ? " asked the counsel for the defence.

The witness. — " Somewhat."

" Do you take an oath or oaths ? "

The witness. — " Yes, sir."

" Do you take those on the Bible, a crucifix, or with uplifted hand ? "

The witness. — " I won't answer that question. This is a secret order."

The defence wished to show that these oaths were taken with great solemnity on the crucifix.

The court said : " I should be very reluctant to force a man to reveal anything of this kind. I assume you don't want the juror, and I think he had better not sit."

The counsel for the defence then asked the juror if he had taken certain oaths, reading the form of such oaths from a newspaper. The witness declined to answer, and was not compelled to. He was challenged, and was excused by the court.

Another juror refused to give the name of the order to which he belonged, presumptively the " A. P. A."

"What reason can you give, juror, why you should not state the name of the order?" asked the Court.

" I am obligated not to tell."

" I understood you to say," said the counsel for the prosecution, " that you did not object to stating the principles of the order. Now, will you tell me what those principles are?"

" There are two principles. One is to support the national government, and the other is to cast a vote but once, and to have that vote counted as cast."

The Court. — " Those principles are very proper. There is certainly nothing to object to in either."

The juror said that there were no other principles generally sustained by the organization. The two he had mentioned were the vital principles on which the order was founded.

The following dialogue occurred between a juror and the counsel for the defence, —

" Did you take an oath to oppose all Catholics?"

" I did not."

" Did you take an oath not to employ Catholics when you could secure Protestants ? "

" I did not."

" You took no such oath ? "

" There are two kinds of Catholics, — Holy Catholics and Roman Catholics."

" And you are opposed to the Roman ? "

" Well, I must say I am."

" Have you taken an oath to oppose them ? "

" I don't remember."

" What was in the oath you took ? "

" I decline to answer the question."

The attempt to classify Robert Ross as a bigot was a failure. He was a Protestant and a Presbyterian, and therefore not a Roman Catholic. He believed in an absolute separation of church and state, in a free church, a free press, free schools. He did not favor the appropriation of public funds for sectarian institutions ; nor would he countenance a division of the school funds between Protestants and Romanists. These are American principles. Inasmuch as he and the remainder of the male members of the family were not connected with the secret society in question, neither he nor they can be justly accused of any demerits attributed to it. The society is not a part of his personal or family history, except as abortive attempts were made to make it appear so. It exists in Troy, and has members in the thirteenth ward. A sufficient proportion of jurymen acknowledged membership in it to create the impression that it is numerically strong in that city and in Rensselaer County.

CHAPTER IX.

Y. P. S. C. E. *versus* MUNICIPAL MISRULE.

THE Twelfth International Convention of the Young People's Society of Christian Endeavor was held in Montreal, July, 1893. It represented 26,284 societies and 1,577,040 members distributed over the globe. Rev. F. E. Clark, D.D., the founder of the original society, and the President of the United Society, presided over the Convention, and delivered his annual address. He advocated not political partisanship, but a larger and more intelligent spirit of patriotism and good citizenship. The Montreal Convention was attended by about seventeen thousand delegates; and President Clark's message to them was : —

"Go to the primaries of your party, and take your Christian Endeavor pledge with you. Go to the caucus; get into the legislature; stand for Congress or for Parliament; but, when you get there, for God and the church and your country do what *He* would like to have you do."

At the time that this address was delivered Robert Ross was not a member of an Endeavor Society. None existed in the church to which he belonged. But he was a member of all the leading spiritual organizations of young people that did exist in the church and in the city. Those organizations maintained and executed, separately, one or more of the principles of the Christian Endeavor Society. The Young People's Unions and the Y. M. C. A. and the Brotherhood of Andrew and Philip stood for denominational loyalty, inter-denominational fellowship, and systematic committee work. The A. and P. Brotherhood stood for definite, pledged service. In spirit, therefore, Robert was an Endeavorer before a society was formed in Oakwood Presbyterian Church.

He did not need such advice as President Clark gave. He was accustomed to go to the caucus, the primary meeting. He did not seek office. The advice of President Clark was not intended to provoke offensive office-seeking. But he did seek, at all hazards, even at the risk and sacrifice of his life, a pure ballot. He was a self-sacrificing patriot. He was in Scranton, Penn., during the

week previous to the election in Troy, but he
came home expressly to vote and to protect the
polls from repeaters. His creed, the creed of all
good citizens, was well expressed in the notice
that was posted, March 9, on the doors of William
H. Frear's Bazaar : —

"Every man should have the right to vote
peaceably once, and have it counted fairly and
honestly. The bazaar will be closed from two to
four P.M. to-day in honor of the memory of Robert
Ross."

If he had not suffered martyrdom, the Society
of Christian Endeavor of the Oakwood Church
at the close of the year would have had something definite to report at its own meeting, and
to the Thirteenth Annual Convention of World-
wide Christian Endeavor, Cleveland, O., July 11–
15. After his death one of his associates in the
Brotherhood of Andrew and Philip said, " He was
worth any six of us, and he was worth any six of
us at the polls."

As has already been noted, an Endeavor Society
was organized in Oakwood Church, exactly mid-
way between the International Montreal Convention and the local March election where Ross's

life ended. These facts explain why a mass-meeting of the Young People's Societies of Christian Endeavor, of Troy and vicinity, was held Sunday, March 18, in the same Presbyterian and Baptist churches that had held the citizens' meetings on Thursday evening, March 8, and the mourners at the funeral, March 9. Four great audiences assembled within that one month to honor the memory and perpetuate the influence of Robert Ross. They had distinguishing and unique characteristics. The audience of Thursday evening was an audience of men ; the audience of Friday was an audience of kindred, friends, societies, and city officials ; the audience of Sunday, March 18, was an audience of young people, that met at their respective churches and proceeded to the union meeting in a body ; the audience in Music Hall, Monday afternoon, March 26, when the Memorial Association was formed, was an audience of ladies.

The Endeavor mass-meeting was opened with a song service led by Joseph Knight, after which Harvey S. McLeod, who presided, welcomed the societies in behalf of the Young People's Christian Union of the Second Presbyterian Church, in whose edifice they were assembled.

The principal address of the occasion was delivered by the Rev. Herbert C. Hinds, pastor of Adam Ross, 2d, and John C. Ross, two of the four brothers who defended the rights of American citizens so bravely. The wonder is that they escaped wounds and death when the fifteen or twenty shots were fired promiscuously in the encounter that occurred. Their membership is in the Ninth Presbyterian Church ; and they had long been accustomed to good preaching of patriotism and Christian citizenship from the Rev. N. B. Remick, D.D., who was pastor of that church from 1869 to 1891, a period of twenty-two years, that covered and paralleled nearly the whole life of Robert Ross.

Pastor Hinds asked and answered the question : —

" What can the Young People's Societies do for municipal reform ? "

He said in part :

"I would rather stand before you on this platform, on this occasion, than before any number of crowned heads of Europe on a state occasion. . . . To be content simply to denounce a wrong and to stop there will be of little practical service.

We must prosecute the cases against criminals
in high and low places to the bitter end, and leave
nothing undone which will bring the guilty before
the bar of justice and behind the bars of the
prison. . . . When I see the church smiling
complacently and comparatively inactive in the
presence of perils compared with which the Goths
and Vandals who threatened ancient Rome are
not to be mentioned ; when I know that Christian
pastors beseech in vain for their prosperous members to do anything adequate for the purging of
our municipal affairs ; when I see men whose fortunes are measured by the miles, and whose gifts
for worthy objects are computed in inches ; when
I see the sink-holes of corruption into which our
young men and women are dropping by hundreds
and thousands, and remember that we find it impossible to open an adequate number of reading-
rooms and coffee-rooms where the temptations
are the mightiest and deadliest, then I must believe
that hiring a pew in a church, saying our prayers
morning and evening, or hearing a sermon on the
Sabbath, is not the whole duty of a good citizen
and a Christian man, whether young or old.

"It has often been said that the Sunday-school
movement is the most important organization in
Christian history ; but after a careful reflection I
regard the rise, the marvellous growth, of the
Young People's Christian Unions, the Young People's Baptist Unions, the Epworth Leagues, and
the Christian Endeavor Societies, as the most
important events in the annals of the church.

Young friends, you represent organizations which can completely overthrow vice and crime within the boundaries of this Empire State, and drive the arch-conspirators into retirement and disgrace. . . . Teach young children to hate the saloons. We must not allow any shadow to obscure the resplendent scene of freedom on God's holy day. We will not permit in these days of triumph any influence to desecrate the Christian Sabbath. Worse than our great liquor traffic, worse than our political corruption, worse than the menace of our criminal population, is the lethargy of the best classes of our people, of the American born and bred citizens of our land. The soldiers of the Grand Army of the Republic, more than a quarter of a century ago, shouldered muskets and drew swords in behalf of our country. And now Post Griswold, G. A. R., re-enlists as a regiment in the grand army of righteousness. . . . And as long as the Hudson shall flow or the Atlantic roll, so long as the violet shall speak of modesty, or the rose tell of love, so long as there shall be the appreciation of the manly, the lovely and divine in human action, so long will the influence of our hero's life be felt on the heart for the purity of the ballot."

While efforts were making to secure a jury for the trial of Shea, curiously enough the name of Lawrence Sheary, brewer, was called, just as Doring's band came marching past the Court

House, playing "Onward, Christian Soldiers," the favorite rallying and marching hymn of the Endeavor Society. The juxtaposition of the brewer, the hymn, and the society may serve to note that the society is opposed to the brewery.

However Robert's life is viewed, it seems to touch the annals and memorials of patriotism. He went to Cleveland, O., immediately after the revolver caucus in February. In that city is the splendid monument to Garfield, with whom as a martyr to bad politics he has been compared. Likewise he has been compared with Lovejoy, Lincoln, and Ellsworth, of kindred history. The business letters that he wrote from Cleveland, February 9 and 10, contained allusions to the then recent revolver caucus. A disturbance occasioned by a drunken "drummer" reminded him of it. In referring to a motor that he had put in the First Baptist Church of Cleveland, he wrote : "She went off at 'the drop of the hat.'" He had acquired the expression from some Roman Catholic priest. It means "instantly" or "quickly." It refers to the signal used between the parties in a contest. When the hat drops the struggle begins at once.

How little he realized then that his native city during the next month would be kindled into admiration and mourning for him, and into fury against his murderer and the impelling forces inducing it ; and that within less than six months the city where he then was would be honoring his memory, sounding his praises, and planning to perpetuate his influence through the representatives of more than two million Endeavorers in all lands on the globe.

President Clark, unable to attend the Cleveland Endeavor Convention, sent to it and to the writer a message in recognition of Robert as the first martyr of the Endeavor Society. Secretary Baer, in his annual report, expressed the history and the prospect as follows : —

"Our good-citizenship campaign has cultivated a greater and more intelligent spirit of patriotism and Christian citizenship everywhere, and has been fearlessly waged, even to the sacrifice of the life of one of our own comrades. But Bat Shea's victim, Robert Ross of Troy, cruelly murdered at the voting-booth, doing his duty, still lives ; and we press on over his body to catch his spirit, determined in the right to put to flight Bat Sheas everywhere, whether it be in Troy, Boston, Chi-

cago, New York, or in the remotest hamlet over
which the Stars and Stripes or the Union Jack
swing their peaceful folds. God save America!
God save England! God save the world!"

At the session on Friday morning, July 13, an
Open Parliament was held for answers to the
question, "What has your Society done to promote good citizenship?" It was conducted by
Edwin D. Wheelock of Chicago, Ill. There was
also a presentation to societies of diplomas
awarded by the United Society for best work
reported in promoting good citizenship.

The Golden Rule, in reporting the proceedings
of this session, said : —

"In snappy sentences the year's glorious work
is shouted out, — saloons put down, Sunday laws
enforced, gambling suppressed, the poor aided,
good-citizenship rallies, pledges of better citizenship, unions organized, elections carried, anti-
tobacco laws passed, and, alas! one Christian
Endeavor martyr to the cause of good-citizenship,
Robert Ross of Troy, N.Y., shot at the polls."

The Rev. W. R. Taylor, D.D., of Rochester,
N.Y., in presenting the diplomas, referred in fitting terms to the reasons why one was awarded to

the society in Oakwood Avenue Church in Troy. The President of that society, F. Bunce, and Leroy Collins, President of the Local Union, were requested to rise and receive the Chautauqua salute. The great tent, seating ten thousand people, rang with applause. The Rev. Graham Taylor, D.D., of Chicago, proposed that Robert Ross Good Citizenship Committees should be organized.

The Rev. Rufus W. Miller of Hummelstown, Penn., the founder of the Andrew and Philip Brotherhood, attended the Endeavor Convention, and at a fraternal meeting in the Y. M. C. A. building referred to Robert in suitable terms. Three organizations were represented, directly or indirectly, in the service, and Robert was a member of all of them, — the Endeavor Society, the Brotherhood, and the Y. M. C. A.

Christian citizenship was one of several leading themes of the Cleveland Convention. The Rev. Smith Baker, D.D., of East Boston, Mass., in one of the addresses said : "Any intimidation at the polls is a crime against democracy." If this be true, what shall be said of foul, brutal murder, and attempts at murder, at the polls ? Dr. Baker enumerated five conditions of Chris-

tian citizenship, all of which prevailed in the
life of Robert Ross, — "Intelligence, impartial-
ity, righteousness, independence, and conscien-
tiousness."

The Rev. H. B. Grose of Chicago, in a similar
vein, said : —

"Election bribery and ballot-box stuffing must
stop in order that free government may go on."

Frank Leslie's Weekly, which discussed repeatedly the murder of Robert Ross, in its issue for
July 26 published an editorial on "Religion and
Good Citizenship," in the conclusion of which,
after detailing the facts in an Endeavor crusade
against the saloon in a city suburban to New
York, said : "This is citizenship at its best, and
the organization which nourishes such a spirit,
incarnating itself in positive acts in political as
well as moral relations, must rank as a foremost
force in our modern life."

CHAPTER X.

OFFICIALS AS SPOILSMEN AND FREEBOOTERS.

THE evidence is cumulative that the one-man power in Troy has been injurious and pervasive. It has debased many, if not all, departments of the city government. It has been exerted for a decade and a half.

This volume is patriotic as distinct from partisan. Robert Ross was more patriotic than partisan.

> "The Right shall live, while Faction dies !
> All traitors draw a fleeting breath;
> But patriots drink from God's own eyes
> Truth's light that conquers Death ! "

The bench is supposed to be non-partisan. Judge Lewis E. Griffith, a resident of Troy, and Judge of the County Court and Court of Sessions, was formerly District Attorney. Politically he has been an ally of Senator Murphy. In charging the grand jury, May 12, 1894, he said : —

"You will be called upon to inquire of crimes committed in this county which have done more harm and positive injury to the city of Troy and its interests than if scourged with pestilence or afflicted with famine — crimes which strike a death-blow to the vital principles of free government; which set at naught the will of a sovereign people, and allow the damnable, wicked, lawless actions of a mob to voice the sentiments of an outraged public. . . .

" Both of the great political parties are charge-able with a dereliction of duty in failing to prose-cute offenders against election laws."

Judge Griffith gave a list of particulars in proof of his statement, and added : —

"Upon examining the records of the United States District Court, I find that not five per cent of the persons arraigned by the commissioners for offences against the election laws have been indicted and tried. . . .

" There has been a disregard of duty by grand jurors and public officers in dealing with this species of crime. There has been no sincere effort made by either of the great political parties to suppress it, or punish offenders. There seems to have been a tacit understanding between both parties that offenders against the ballot would not be considered criminal ; yet occasionally some offender would be indicted in the federal courts, where a fine of a few dollars would be imposed, upon a plea of guilty, while others would pass through the ordeal of waiting about the court-room for a jury to pronounce them guiltless."

This is the language of confession and accusation. It is non-partisan to the extent that it excuses neither of the two leading parties, and accuses both. It is not our purpose to arbitrate and decide which of the two parties is the more guilty in violating election laws and in failing to prosecute offenders. The city officials for years have been chiefly, if not exclusively, Democrats. The county officials have been Democrats and Republicans. The charge, as quoted, is a part of the history, and, as such, it is reproduced.

Officials are accustomed to use more than a reasonable discretion what laws they will enforce. They are legally liable for the violation of some laws that are explicit, mandatory, and prohibitory. District Attorney Kelly is to be tried in October for alleged inefficiency, before a commission appointed by Governor Flower.

While the trial of " Bat " Shea was in progress, Judge Williams said : —

"When I came here, I found that of all the court officers appointed by the sheriff, not one was a constable as provided by the statute. . . . I find it has been the custom to appoint any one, whether he be a constable or not. It is about time that the sheriff understood the statute. . . . I have been warned from a variety of sources that trustworthy court officers are difficult to obtain in this county."

The bearing of these facts on the trial of Shea was that his conviction for a capital offence by a jury in charge of unqualified and disqualified court officers would have been valueless in law.

During the trial, some prisoners escaped from the Troy jail, a not infrequent occurrence. Shea was conveyed to Clinton Prison, Dannemora, Friday, July 13. The chances of his escape from prison were thereby reduced.

During the first week in July, a committee of the State Senate instituted an investigation into the police department of Troy. The Committee of One Hundred for Public Safety had employed a detective of the New York Society for the Prevention of Crime, of which the Rev. Charles H. Parkhurst, D.D., is the famous and efficient president. The testimony showed not merely mutual confidence and co-operation between the New York society and the Troy committee, but proof

The Troy Jail.

Published in the Troy Times. Reproduced by permission.

of kindred crimes by the New York and Troy
police. Reliable testimony and sufficient evidence
were furnished to demonstrate that the police are
accustomed to coerce disorderly houses as to
their purchases of furniture, liquors, and cigars ;
to furnish such houses protection for a financial
consideration amounting to a regular tax and
license ; to borrow money from the keepers with
no expectation of or demand for repayment ; to
use these houses as refuges when intoxicated ; to
retain the money of persons arrested or held as
witnesses ; and to exact subscriptions for gifts.

The clerk of the board of excise testified as
follows : —

" The money collected [from disorderly houses]
was paid over to the charity board. I made such
collections because it was a custom established
by my predecessors. Molloy, Magill, and O'Neil
were the commissioners. [The Commissioner
Molloy referred to is the present Mayor of Troy,
a cousin of Senator Murphy.] They did not
direct me to make such collections; but they knew
that I did so, as the entries were made in the
books. In these cases no licenses were issued, as
the law would not allow the issuing of licenses to
disreputable houses. The board regarded these
houses as disreputable houses. A previous board

of some years back had refused to grant licenses
to such houses.

" These collections were paid to the chamber-
lain for the support of the poor.   As long as they
were selling liquor," said the witness, " they ought
to pay for it, as much as some poor widow down
town."

" Don't you know," asked Attorney Frank S.
Black, " that they had no right to sell liquor ? "

" I don't suppose that they had any right to
sell," replied the witness.

" Do you know of any law that allows you to
receive money from those people ? " asked Mr.
Black.

" I do not," replied the witness.   " I knew in
receiving money that they intended to sell liquor."

" You knew that you were receiving this money
in violation of law, did you not ? " asked Mr.
Black.

" No, I did not," replied the witness.

" What else was this money you received except
hush money ? "

" I don't know as you'd call it hush money."

" Do you know of any other purpose for which
the money was received except to violate the
law ? "

" No, sir."

One of the witnesses before the investigating
committee was John Ross, who, by request of a
representative of Senator Murphy, called at his

brewery, March 5, the day preceding the death of Robert. William Ross accompanied John, and during the trial of McGough testified to the facts of the interview as follows : —

"At the brewery we met Senator Murphy and Police Commissioner Molloy, who was a candidate for mayor. . . . John told how he had been assaulted at the caucus, and showed where he had been struck in the face with a revolver, and told Murphy how Shea, Cleary, Owen Judge, and other Democrats of the thirteenth ward, had broken up our caucus. We asked Murphy and Molloy to send us policemen on election day, who would not assist repeaters to vote. . . . We also told Murphy how a policeman had thrown our brother Robert out of the polling-place in the third district of the thirteenth ward at the fall election. . . . Murphy said, 'There will not be a repeater in the city to-morrow;' and we thought that he and Molloy could give us the protection we wanted."

Senator Murphy, it will be seen, tacitly assumed that he could control the presence or absence of repeaters. If he had used his restraining power, and kept his word, the fatality of election day would not have occurred, and William Ross, his caller of March 5, would not have suffered deafness for life from a pistol shot and a bullet wound

in the neck. The very things occurred against
which John and William Ross tried to guard,
because they had occurred before; viz., repeaters
were present, armed with firearms, and policemen
who knew and aided them. Senator Murphy is a
monarch without legal standing or accountability
as a political manager.

In opening for the defence, in the trial of
McGough, Attorney Norton located a part of the
responsibility for the situation when he addressed
the jury as follows : —

"I have heard of repeating in this city ever
since I was a boy. For more than fifteen years
the most flagrant outrages on the rights of
citizens on election day have been permitted to
go unpunished. At every election these offences
against the sacredness of the ballot-box have been
countenanced. Repeaters have operated, and
ballot-boxes have been stuffed. We know, the
prosecution knows, and you can guess, where
the blame lies; and if the prosecution does not
desire to place the blame where it belongs, and to
place the responsibility for all these outrages, I
shall assert, gentlemen, that it is not honest to
try to place it all upon poor McGough and poor
Shea. Crime upon crime against a fair ballot has
been perpetrated in this city for years; but I
never heard of an effort to put an end to these

crimes until the blood of brave Robert Ross aroused the authorities to the necessity of making some sort of a front. They are not honest, I tell you, in this prosecution, nor in the effort to prosecute Shea. . . . It is the prosecuting officers of this city and county who should bear this fearful responsibility, and not Shea, not McGough. I protest against this effort to make them the sole responsible parties. If they were engaged in repeating, it was not as principals, but as tools of others high and prominent in position."

We have said that the evidence is cumulative, as bearing upon the evil doings of "the powers that be," and of the supreme power behind all the thrones in the government of Troy that asserts itself in the county also, and in the State and in the nation. The testimony before the Senate Committee and in the trial of McGough, relating to the police, was confirmatory of that given at the trial of Shea; for during the trial an inspector of elections, James H. Crutchley, gave a graphic account of the manner in which a crowd of fifteen or twenty repeaters, inclusive of Shea and Mc-Gough, crowded into the door of the polling-place, ignoring the regular line of voters, and voted, swearing in their votes because challenged. They

held in sight the slips given them, containing the
registered names on which they were to vote.
They withdrew for fifteen or twenty minutes,
then came back and voted a second time, giving
different names.   Again they crowded in ahead
of the regular line.   Police officer Patrick Cahill
had charge of the regular line of voters.   Cahill
pushed the regular line back, so as to let the
crowd of unregistered strangers in to get their
ballots.   The officer told the regular voters, said
the witness, that he would "break some of their
heads if they didn't keep still."

"What position did this man hold — patrol-
man?" asked Justice Williams.

"Yes, sir," replied the witness.

"Is he still on the force?"

"I believe he is."

The inquiry of Justice Williams was the inquiry
of surprise and astonishment.   No other interpre-
tation of it reasonably can be made.

Jeremiah Cleary took voters from the regular
line by seizing them by the collar and pulling
them off the steps leading to the polling-place.
Shea and his gang voted early and often in different districts for half of election day, and appar-

ently would have voted late and often, and so filled
out the day, if they had not been dispersed by the
collision of forces that resulted in murder, and
narrowly escaped resulting in a plurality of mur-
ders. Arthur E. Bartlett, a Prohibitionist watcher,
testified as follows : —

"I heard one of the men give my name and
residence, and I challenged him, but he swore his
vote in.   I called the attention of the inspectors
to the fact that I was the only person of the name
living at the number given.   I was personally ac-
quainted with two of the inspectors, Crutchley
and Thomas Bohan.   When the gang had voted I
went out to follow the stranger who voted on my
name.   He went directly across the street to
McClure's saloon.   I continued to watch this
stranger ten or fifteen minutes."

This testimony is exactly similar to that of Mr.
Armstrong which has already been quoted.   Mr.
Bartlett, when the stranger voted on his name,
called upon an officer to arrest the offender; but
the officer refused.

Likewise, in the trial of McGough for shooting
William Ross, Ernest V. Perry, an inspector of
elections on the day of the shooting, testified that
he had known times in the thirteenth ward when

sixty illegal votes had been received by the inspectors.   "Why, last fall," said the witness,
"twenty-five illegal votes were cast in the third
district alone.   Duncan C. Kaye challenged every
one of them, too, and the inspectors paid no attention to him, other than to administer what they
called an oath before receiving the ballots."

"Did you ever make complaint to the District
Attorney about this?" asked Mr. Hitt, counsel for
the defence.

"Yes, sir."

"When?"

"When I was called before the grand jury."

How much security and safety there will be on
election days, or by night throughout the year,
under the so-called protection of the police, we
leave our readers to infer.

CHAPTER XI.

CIVIL SERVICE REFORM IMPERATIVE.

IN the July, 1894, number of the *Century Magazine*, an unsigned article was published under the heading "Topics of the Time," entitled " A Martyr of To-day." Robert Ross was the martyr meant. The writer, a member of the *Century* staff of editors, left no doubt of the bearing, in his judgment, of the two sides of the history of this sad case, the bad side and the good. He summarized both in the following paragraph : —

" The death of Ross in the discharge of the highest duty of citizenship has revealed to the American people an example of civic devotion and of self-sacrifice which should inspirit decent citizens everywhere, while it should startle the indifferent into a realization of the desperate and dangerous character of the new generation of political spoilsmen.

" Robert Ross was in an eminent sense a martyr to liberty. No man that fell at Lexington or Sumter gave his life to his country with more willingness or for a better principle."

This paragraph recalls the fact that when Robert was leaving home on election morning, his mother expressed apprehension of trouble during the day; and he answered that some one must take a stand for the rights of the people. This sentiment was wrought into floral emblems at his funeral.

Likewise, the editor discerned and appropriately characterized the true nature of the two antagonisms in Troy and in many other cities. The collision is not between the representatives of two or more political parties that differ, however radically, about the principles and policies of general or local self-government. There is a problem in such conditions, but not a menace. The very genius of our government and institutions provides for such honorable and honest contention, and confides securely in the outcome.

But the hostility that is dangerous is that which issues from the vicious and the criminal, who not only do the illegal, but the controlling thing, and determine the result of the election.

Assistant District Attorney Fagan, in his opening address to the jury, in the trial of McGough for shooting William Ross, said : —

"Murder involves the taking of human life through malice ; but in this case there is something dearer than a single life — it is the question of American citizenship, a question which comes home to us all, Democrats and Republicans, rich and poor. The question is whether it is the good citizen with the ballot, or the thug with his revolver, who shall control our nation."

It was only by one chance in ten thousand that McGough was not tried on a charge of murder. A slight variation in the course of the bullet and it would have penetrated the brain.

It has been asserted in the progress of this narrative that the normal and legal results of elections have not only been changed, but nullified and reversed. The case is "Shea *versus* Ross," "The Criminal *versus* the Citizen," "Fraud and Violence *versus* Honesty and Self-Defence." If it be decided, partly or wholly, in favor of the pistol politician, then danger has already become disaster. The writer in *The Century*, said : —

"The danger of the ascendancy of the criminal element in politics is a danger to men of all parties, and there is hardly a city of the United States where there is not need of a non-partisan body of picked men whose duty it shall be to exalt the sanctity of the now degraded suffrage ;

to agitate for the most perfect election laws, and
for more severe penalties for their violation; to
bring the force of public opinion to bear on the
selection of registry and election boards; to scan
and purify the lists of voters; to study the rights
of citizens at elections, and to defend them at the
polls; to become familiar with the *personnel* of
the districts in which they are to serve as watchers, and to exert the whole power of the law on
election day to insure the free casting and faithful
counting of the vote. An appropriate name for
such a body would be 'The Robert Ross Association.' . . .

"The imprisonment of twenty-nine offenders
against the election law in New York City was
accomplished by exactly the sort of work which
might be undertaken by these associations. Bearing the name of Robert Ross, they would at once
be a challenge to evil-doers, and a solemn procla-
mation of the serious nature of their mission."

Civil service reform is too large a question to
be discussed in the brief limits of this chapter or
biography. But the bearings of it in this case
may be shown after the *Century* writer has been
allowed to express himself as to the necessity for
it : —

"The Spoils System is a deadly upas-tree
which the nation has long been nourishing; its
leaves are dropping upon us as never before; here

and there we have broken a twig or lopped off a branch; but the time has come to root it up entirely. To do this in nation, state, city, and village, is a purpose to which every good citizen should devote himself. The death of Robert Ross will not have been in vain if it shall lead his countrymen to ponder the fundamental principle for which he died."

Evidently there are, to say the least, two departments of city government which have figured in the preceding narrative that ought to be divorced absolutely from politics, — the school and the police departments. It is revolting that a school-teacher or the friend of a school-teacher should need to consult or depend upon a professional politician for his or her position; and in Troy that the teacher should suffer the humiliation of consultation with and dependence upon a brewer boss. He or she thereby becomes the subject, not of Republican and Democratic government, not of an aristocracy, as government by the best or the few, but of a monarchy, the government of one, and the one, we repeat and emphasize, a generator of saloons!

It is even more revolting that the policeman should owe his office to personal and offensive, if

not corrupt, politics and politicians; that he should
be the appointee and tool of one or a few rather
than the impartial, incorruptible representative
and defender of all; that he should account for
himself to the politician, not to the public. The
policeman who does not protect the polls and
good citizens; who does not terrorize, and, when
the conditions require, arrest the political assassin
and repeater, is himself a criminal, and one of the
worst conceivable. He is comparable only to the
father who dishonors and slays his daughter; he
ranks with the anarchist who would destroy
society, and perpetuate disorder, brutality, and
civil war; with the marauder and brigand who
makes a child his victim. He should be rail-
roaded out of office and power into prison.

The police of Troy were efficient and shrewd
enough to arrest and imprison an innocent man
for the murder of Robert Ross, John H. Boland,
and to keep him in jail until the coroner's inquest
was completed.

When he was released, a group of fifty prominent citizens escorted him from the jail to his
home, displaying profusely the Stars and Stripes.

Rev. E. B. Olmstead, of Delevan, N.Y., has

Hon. Galen R. Hitt.

invented an automatic ballot cabinet, the use of which has been made optional by the State legislature for towns and villages. Efforts will be put forth to make its use compulsory. It provides a private gallery about four feet square, that shuts in the voter from observers. As he enters, a guard or inspector's clerk furnishes him with a ball, which he drops into an orifice of "ballot distributers" plainly marked "Democrat," "Republican," "Prohibition." If he cannot read, he sees party emblems, — an "eagle," a "flag," a "white ribbon," a "sheaf of grain," etc., one of which, he has been instructed, indicates his party.

He then pulls a knob, and a ticket or set of tickets is automatically thrust out of the machine. He passes through an exit door, and deposits a straight ticket in the ballot-box, or enters a booth to change his ticket. Straight ticket voting will be so rapid that very many less voting precincts will be needed. More than one thousand votes may be cast in a day.

In each of the party ballot distributers there is a numbering device, so that every vote is registered as a ticket or set of tickets is delivered ; and the moment the knob is pulled out the unlocking ball rolls out through the machine to the guard.

The closing of the doors of the respective ticket cases in the ballot distributers shuts from view the registers ; and on opening these doors at the close of the election the result thereof is shown by the automatic count.   The law provides that in case the inspectors find in the ballot-boxes at the close of the election more tickets of either party than are indicated by the party register, they shall be rejected.

The invention secures secrecy of the ballot, registers the straight ticket vote of each party, prevents an erroneous canvass of the votes cast, and does away with electioneering by ticket peddling.   Each voter can get only one ballot or set of ballots.

On the wall of the private cabinet is a kodac or snapshot device which watchers may operate so as to make it a " Repeater Catcher."   We might call it in derision of him a substitute for the Trojan policeman; and in praise, a substitute for Robert Ross.

CHAPTER XII.

REDEMPTION OF THE CITY THE GOAL OF CIVIC LIFE.

THE life of Robert Ross has been considered in itself and in its public relations. It is now practically concluded. This is not a history of Troy, except in part. Otherwise a very different story might be told, which has been suggested incidentally and occasionally. The history covers more than a century, and down to the close of the Civil War, or 1865-70, it is a history of which any city in the land might be proud ; a history of enterprise, of industrial energy and success, of an educational centre, inclusive of a commercial college, an academy, a female seminary, a theological seminary, a school for civil engineers, and a popular debating society and library. It is a history of pioneer work, of public spirit, and private beneficence. The change has come, and the changed reputation, within a score of years. But the change, great as it is, is not complete. Through public appropriations and private gifts, since 1880, a monument has been raised (in co-operation with the county) to the soldiers and sailors of the war of 1861–65 ; a Young Woman's Home has been founded; a Railroad Y. M. C. A. has been organized ; a Memorial Chapel, with incinerating apparatus of the most approved construction, has been erected in Oakwood Cemetery ; the centennial of the city (1889) has been worthily observed, and a new life given on the same site to the Troy Female Seminary, long famous under the management of Madame Emma Willard. New churches have been organized, and many of the older edifices reconstructed and refurnished. A new and splendid orphan asylum is soon to be entered, a new high school, a new public library. It would be a pleasure to give details, inclusive of the names of donors, but our limits will not permit. The history of Troy as a Pergamum, a Sardis, a Laodicea, is confined to about two decades, so far as there is justification for so considering it ; and its reputation as such, in spite of the record made herein, is worse than its character. Its politics, elective

and appointive, affecting all departments of municipal affairs, the enactment and execution of
municipal law, and the administration of justice
and local government, have been the prime causes
of the revolution that has occurred. The conditions created by indiscriminate, unrestricted im-
migration, easy naturalization, and the licensed
saloon have given the professional politician, the
boss politician, and the briber, *silver and golden*
opportunities, of which they have been quick to
avail themselves.

Troy is a typical American city, in most re-
spects, in its history during the last generation.
It is a crucial city now, and will remain so for a
long term, in its tested capacity for municipal reforms. It represents alike the cities of the first and
second rank, — New York, Philadelphia, Boston,
Chicago, and Brooklyn on the one hand ; and on
the other, Buffalo, Albany, Pittsburgh, Baltimore,
and similar cities. In it is every problem that
faces the American people, calling for the dif-
fusion of religion, morality, intelligence, education,
honesty, truthfulness, and kindred virtues ; and
the abolition of irreligion, immorality, ignorance,
race prejudice, caste, and sectarianism ; the eradi-

cation of the criminal by penal and reformatory
agencies. The problems exist in Troy in a radical,
aggravated, intrenched form ; but in some form
and degree they are distributed through all, or
nearly all, American cities. The largest cities are
worse than Troy and the cities of the second rank,
in the extent of their slums and the social degra-
dation of their tenements and " foreign " quarters.
The antagonisms between Protestants and Roman Catholics in Troy, as elsewhere, disclose two
schools of Protestants and two wings of Catholicism. There is a self-styled liberal school of
Protestants that believes it finds its affinity in
a similar school of Catholics ; and these two
trust each other, co-operate in emergencies and in
things common, such as antagonism to the saloon,
the preservation of a quiet Sabbath, and the enforcement of law. There is a school of Protestants and a school of Catholics that represent
the survival and continuance, not the cessation, of
hereditary historical bias and antagonisms. The
collision has been transferred from the Old World
to the New. It is the facts, the history, the conditions, with which we are dealing, not their
equities.

A distinction is to be made between a problem and a peril. A problem may be perpetuated without becoming a peril. Even a disease of the heart may not be organic, but functional. A man, William Ross for example, may be wounded, and his life tremble in the balance, yet he may survive the emergency, and carry the ball, not yielding to death, nor to more serious chronic invalidism than deafness. Likewise a city, a State, a nation. American cities have become deteriorated by social ills, demanding acute treatment, drastic remedies, civic and moral surgery; but these cities and evils are more problematic than perilous. Sober study of the lessons of history, and close observation of the recuperative tendencies of recent years, and of the ultimate power of choice remnants of population, American and adopted, are the reasons for our civic creed. Counsellor Raines, addressing the jury in the trial of McGough, and referring to the election misdeeds in Troy, said : —

" There is a power and a whip in almost every city of the country which suppresses these transactions."

We would change his statement from the present into the future tense. In the conclusion of that trial, when applause was awarded to the counsel for the defence by friends of the prisoner, Justice Williams suppressed it, and uttered reformatory sentiment when he said : —

" You may carry on, in the sort of courts you have been in the habit of visiting, but you cannot do it in this court."

Likewise Counsellor Raines commended the citizens who assembled at the polls in the third precinct of the thirteenth ward of Troy, March 6, and said : —

" There stood seventy-five as good men as live in Rensselaer or any other county."

The seventy-five in that precinct, and the Committee of One Hundred appointed seventy-two hours later, were representative, typical. Their testimony and their deeds have not only convicted Shea, but McGough, who has been sentenced to the State prison for nineteen years and six months, whose sentence may be reduced by good behavior to less than twelve years. They have cornered

Senator Murphy, testifying that he gave a guaranty for the action and absence of repeaters, the value of which, in fact, proved to be the equivalent of a promise to secure their presence. The reformatory work has begun, but it is by no means ended. The initial steps have been taken which propose to induce members of churches to take a greater interest in Troy's primary meetings and elections. The first meeting was held in the same Presbyterian edifice as the funeral of Robert Ross. Justice Williams, in sentencing McGough, said : —

"One lesson taught to the public is that whatever has been said or may be said about the city of Troy or the county of Rensselaer, honest men are yet strong enough to maintain the law. After the result of these trials they can say, 'We are still strong enough to take care of our own criminals.'"

The churches and minorities in cities should abandon their indifference and lethargy, organize on a non-partisan basis, devote time, labor, and money to purifying, reformatory work ; and by so doing they can and will arrest and nullify, if not abolish, criminality at the polls and associate evils, preliminary and subsequent. Attorney Raines, in

Rochester for twenty-five years, has been an attendant at the opening and closing of the polls. Multiply the one man by many and the system of terrorizing will be reversed. The good citizen will terrorize the bribers and repeaters and ballot-box stuffers.

Rev. Charles Parkhurst, D.D., of New York, after his unique and agonizing experience, says : " I am absolutely confident in my convictions that it is the Church of the living God that has got to take up this matter (municipal reform) and put it through."

Because New York is the Empire State, and New York City is the Metropolis, not only of the State but of the nation, the facts concerning the cities of New York State are typical, and the cities themselves are crucial for reform or a further declension.

In 1846, forty-eight years ago, the population of the State (hundreds omitted) was 2,604,000; that of New York City was 371,000; while the population of all the cities of the State was but 573,000, or about 22 per cent, a little over one-fifth of the entire population of the State. Now the population of the State, according to the last

State census, is 6,513,000; the population of New
York City is 1,801,000; the population of Brooklyn is 995,000; and the population of all of the
cities of the State is 3,987,000, exceeding by 50
per cent the entire population of the State forty-
eight years ago, and constituting 61 per cent of
the present population of the State.

The proposed Greater New York will consist of
the present cities of New York, Brooklyn, Long
Island City, a considerable portion of Queens and
Westchester Counties, and all of Richmond County.
If the present cities of New York and Brooklyn,
and the adjacent territory proposed, are combined
in the Greater New York, that city will start with
a population of 3,000,000; and it is within the
limits of reasonable anticipation and forethought
that before 1915 there will be 5,000,000 people
residing in that great city under a single municipal administration. New York will then be
another London. Outside of and beyond the
Metropolis are the great cities on the lakes, one,
according to the last State census, with 278,000,
and one with 144,000 population; Albany with a
population of 97,000; the contiguous city of Troy
with a population of 64,000; Syracuse with about

92,000; and twenty-eight smaller cities, all with the warrantable expectation of continued development and growth.

New York City has nearly one-third of the population of the State; and the Greater New York, if formed, will have nearly one-half the population of the State. The cities larger than Troy constitute more than half the population of the State, and that preponderance is rapidly increasing. One-half the population of the State is south of the northerly boundary of Yonkers. That population is rapidly increasing, and will ultimately be a part of Greater New York.

The Committee on Cities of the Constitutional Convention of New York, in session during the summer of 1894, from whose report some of the facts in this chapter are taken, reported that : —

"Never before in the history of the world have such prodigious aggregations of people been gathered in cities. Practically it is in this country alone that the great problems they present are to be solved by popular representative government under a written constitution. . . .

"The government of great cities is no longer to be secondary to matters of the State or the nation."

The problems of government, municipal, State, and national, arise largely from the number and quality of saloons; the presence and massing of foreigners who do not speak the English language, and who confound freedom and license; the congestion of population in tenements and slums; the degree of illiteracy, and corruption in politics.

In the city of New York there was, in 1893, one liquor saloon to every 200 persons; but in the slum district, which lies between the business and residential sections, there was one saloon to every 129 persons. The proportion of foreign-born persons in the slums of American cities is very largely in excess of the proportion of the whole population. This excess is in New York 20.35 per cent.

In New York, also, the percentage of illiterates is 1.16 for the entire native-born population, and 14.06 for the foreign-born, the percentage for both being 7.69; while for the slum population the percentage of native-born who are illiterates is 7.20, and of the foreign-born, 57.69, the percentage for both being 46.65.

Of the whole number of voters in New York City, 49.93 per cent are foreign born, while in the slum district 62.44 per cent are foreign born.

Our readers, in view of such awakening, if not alarming facts, will do well to re-read " The Introduction," by the Rev. Josiah Strong, D.D.

We have shown what the crimes against the ballot in Troy have been, and the evident collusion between the criminals and the police. Two criminals have become convicts. The life of one, if sentence is executed, will be taken. The greater criminal in spirit received the less punishment, because less criminal according to the letter of the law. McGough held the brains of the band of repeaters that operated March 6 in the thirteenth ward of Troy. Attorney Raines said that 90 per cent of the blame belonged in reality to him, and 10 per cent to Shea. Justice Williams said to McGough : —

" Your own conduct in these trials has not been in your favor. You are not a good man ; your record is very bad. . . . It is no fault of yours that William Ross does not lie to-day beside his brother Robert in a grave on the hillside."

The officials accused and censured in court, directly and by implication, by the presiding judge and by the attorneys, are impeached at the bar of public opinion ; and self-respect should lead them to demand an investigation or to resign.

Attorney Raines, in addressing the jury in the trial of McGough, said : —

" A collection of bad officers is an example for all times in all communities. The instant your officials become prostituted, the gambling houses and the houses of ill-fame are incorporated in the official system. These evils accumulate, until finally you have that multitudinous system of fraud that was characterized by the Tweed *régime.* So society, from its lowest strata, gradually sees built from the foundation a monster which becomes an incubus to society. And the outcome of all this is what ? Revolution ! "

The kindred crimes at Gravesend in November, 1893, attracted national notice. The facts established in the trial and conviction of the criminals, were that Gravesend had a population, according to the State census, of 8,418 ; its legitimate vote could not exceed 1,600. The events of that election were that sworn officers opened the ballot-boxes and put 2,000 ballots into them. That was done behind a cordon of policemen with club and pistol, barring every one but the conspirators

from the polls, and in so doing defying and resist-
ing the officers of the law and the processes and
mandates of the supreme court.   By such proceedings there was returned and certified a total vote
of 3,672, in a total population of 8,418.   A return
that 600,000 votes had been cast in New York
City, or 50,000 votes in Rochester, would be no
more absurd, and in principle no more dangerous
to the liberties and civil rights of the people.

In other cases, at many other polls of election,
wrongs to the elective franchise similar, though
less flagrant, have been committed.   The Constitutional Convention Committee on Cities, already
quoted, expressed the belief that the danger-point
in our system of government is at the ballot-box,
and that great frauds, exceeding those of stealth
and indirection, can never exist without the com-
plicity of the officers whose duty it is to preserve
order and make arrests ; and affirmed that any
failure of the police to protect the citizen in the
lawful exercise of the elective franchise, whereby
a correct vote is not secured in a given city, such
as Troy or Buffalo, affects not only Rochester,
but every city, every town, and every citizen of
the State.

In the last analysis, therefore, the responsibility for purity and reform is so divided and distributed as to rest upon every citizen, every voter. When it rests upon such citizens as Robert Ross, or his father and brothers, its obligations are discharged, the city and the country are rescued and redeemed. They coveted no higher title than that which belongs to good American citizens. They have been abundantly vindicated in the courts.

In the feudal period of the Middle Ages, when a young man was to be made a knight, the attendants clothed him in a white tunic, a symbol of purity ; in a red robe, the symbol of the blood which he was bound to shed in the service of the faith ; in a toga, — a close black coat, — a symbol of the death which awaited him as well as all men. They put on his coat of mail, bound on his spurs, and girded on his sword. With his helmet on his brow, brandishing his lance, he went forth to war in the contest of chivalry.

When Robert Ross went forth to do his sacred and solemn duty on March 6, and, as the event proved, to sacrifice his life, there was no halo around his head, and he was not clothed in symbolic robes. But, providentially, he had been ordained as a knight of the kingdom of God. As ever, he was plainly but neatly dressed. He wore a dark suit, a light brown overcoat, a Derby hat. The hat was found in the gully in front of the polls with a bullet-hole in the rim. After death his clothes were covered with blood and dirt. There was a bullet-hole in the breast of his overcoat and coat. A bullet had passed through time-tables and memoranda in his pockets, but not through his vest. The exhibit of his clothes was made in court, and it seemed as if his transfigured spirit were present. It is abroad in the church, the State, and the nation, enlisting volunteers in the chivalric strife and patriotic warfare in which, after reaching his majority, he lived and died. We may recall how, in the history of Rome, a wide cleft appeared in the city, dividing it. The oracles were consulted; and the answer was that what constituted the principal strength of the city must be cast into the opening. Curtius, a young knight, decided that manhood was what Rome most revered; and, after having arrayed himself in full armor and mounted his horse, he plunged into the chasm. The people threw after him their offerings and quantities of the fruits of the earth, and the earth closed over him immediately. Robert Ross, the young Trojan knight, in full Christian armor, threw himself into Troy's abyss; and we may believe that since the people at large and the Committee for Safety have added their gifts to his and to those of his father and brothers, Troy's gap has closed. Men who will fill gaps, and throw themselves into the chasms of cities, are the men who in life and in death will redeem our cities and enable us to reach the goal of our civic life.

———————

The following poem, by the editor of *The Century* Magazine, Richard Watson Gilder, kindly furnished in advance of its publication in the magazine, very appropriately closes the record of these pages :

A HERO OF PEACE.

ROBERT ROSS: MURDERED AT THE POLLS, IN TROY, MARCH 6, 1894.

> No bugle on the blast
>   Calls warriors face to face.
> Grim battle being forever past,
>   Gone is the hero-race.
>
> Ah, no ! There is no peace !
>   If liberty shall live,
> Never may freemen dare to cease
>   Their love, their life, to give.

Unto the patriot's heart
  The silent summons comes;
Not braver he who does his part
  To the sound of beating drums.

And thou who gavest youth,
  And life, and all most dear —
Sweet soul, impassionate of truth,
  White on thy murdered bier !

Thy deed, thy date, thy name,
  Are wreathed with deathless flowers;
Thy fate shall be the guiding flame
  That lights to nobler hours.

RICHARD WATSON GILDER.

FINIS.